Ciaran Murtagh is a writer and actor. His first book, *Dinopants*, was published by Piccadilly Press in 2009 and was followed by three sequels. He also writes TV shows and has recently been involved with scripting *The Slammer*, *The 4 O'Clock Club*, *Diddy Movies*, *The Legend of Dick and Dom*, *Scoop*, *Hotel Trubble*, and *Dennis and Gnasher*. He regularly appears in TV shows for CBBC and can be seen in all four series of *The Slammer*.

He lives in London with his wife and secret sweetie cupboard and has a lovely daughter called Eleanor. He is an unapologetic fan of the music of a-ha and still sucks his thumb. It is unclear which of these two facts is more embarrassing to his friends and family.

Other books by Ciaran Murtagh:

Dinopants
Dinopoo
Dinoburps
Dinoball

CIARAN MURTAGH

GENIE IN TRAINING

Illustrated by Adria Meserve

Piccadilly Press • London

For my godson James
– may all your wishes come true,
with or without a genie!
CM

First published in Great Britain in 2012
by Piccadilly Press Ltd,
5 Castle Road, London NW1 8PR
www.piccadillypress.co.uk

A catalogue record for this book is available
from the British Library

ISBN: 978 1 84812 226 0 (paperback)

1 3 5 7 9 10 8 6 4 2

Printed and bound by CPI Group (UK) Ltd, Croydon, CR0 4YY
Cover design by Simon Davis
Cover and interior illustrations by Adria Meserve

CHAPTER 1

'Five, four, three, two, one! You can look now!' said Jamie's dad, who had guided him into the kitchen, his hands over Jamie's eyes.

Jamie Quinn smiled at the sight before him. A *Happy Birthday* banner hung across the window and blue balloons were tied to every chair. Multi-coloured streamers dangled from the lampshade and the kitchen table was covered in sparkles.

Mum was holding a massive birthday cake in the shape of a racing car, Gran was blowing on a bright green party hooter, and Baby Paulie was waddling around the kitchen trying to eat his party hat.

'It's not every day you turn ten,' said Dad, as Jamie looked at a huge pile of presents. 'Now blow out your candles before I call the fire brigade!'

Jamie rolled his eyes. Dad was always making terrible jokes. Mum put the cake on the table. Those ten candles would take some blowing.

'Don't forget to make a wish,' said Gran.

Jamie closed his eyes again, took a deep breath and wished that every day could be his birthday. Then he blew out the candles while everyone clapped and cheered.

While Mum cut the cake, Dad strapped Paulie into his high chair and Jamie gulped down some lemonade. Mum handed him a piece of cake – it was the chocolatiest

chocolate cake he'd ever tasted. It was delicious. Now for the presents!

Jamie always liked to open his birthday presents at tea – he never had time in the morning before school, and this way he could really enjoy himself. There were more than ever this year and it took Jamie ages to open them all. When he'd finished, he was surrounded by lots of wonderful gifts. His favourites were the *Top Gear* DVD his mum and dad had bought him and a big poster of a racing car from Paulie.

'What lovely presents,' said Gran. 'It's a pity I forgot to pop to the shops today – but you've got plenty already.'

Jamie smiled. Gran always pretended she'd forgotten to get him a present – she did it every year. But, in fact, her presents were always absolutely brilliant. Last year she got him a remote controlled robot and the year before that a bumper pack of practical jokes that Jamie used to trick his friends for months.

'Gotcha!' She giggled, rummaging under her chair and pulling out one last present. It was wrapped in gold paper and tied with a blue ribbon. It was a very strange shape and Jamie couldn't think what it might be.

He tugged excitedly at the ribbon and the paper fell away to reveal . . . a teapot.

Jamie's heart sank as he held the battered silver teapot up for everyone to see.

'I knew you'd like it!' said Gran.

Jamie was so disappointed. He knew he shouldn't

mind because he'd got so many other lovely presents, but he'd been really looking forward to Gran's.

'Jamie's very grateful, aren't you, Jamie?' said his mum.

Jamie's mouth opened and closed like a goldfish.

'*Aren't* you, Jamie!' Mum repeated pointedly.

'Oh, yes!' lied Jamie, giving Gran his best false smile. 'It's just what I wanted – it'll, um, be perfect for keeping my football cards in,' he said, while thinking to himself, *That's it. She's finally gone completely tea-potty!*

Later that evening, Jamie said goodnight and carefully carried his presents upstairs. He stuck the poster to his bedroom wall, put the DVD on his shelf and found homes for all of his new toys and games. The only present he didn't know what to do with was the teapot. What had Gran been thinking?

He picked it up and inspected it carefully. It was made of dull silver and was covered in tiny dents and scratches. Jamie tried to take the lid off but it was stuck tight. He peered down the spout. Of course he couldn't see a thing. It would definitely look better if it wasn't so grubby, he decided, so he picked up an old football sock and gave it a good polish.

As soon as he began rubbing, something strange happened. The teapot started wobbling about in his hands!

Jamie dropped it in surprise and gasped as a plume of thick blue smoke poured from the spout. Before long, the smoke was filling his bedroom. Jamie began to cough and splutter. Suddenly there was a large flash.

Jamie rubbed his eyes and stared in disbelief. A pair of twinkling brown eyes were watching him from the other side of the foggy room.

CHAPTER 2

Jamie's mouth dropped open as a tall, thin boy in a waistcoat and pantaloons emerged from the smoke.

The boy flashed him a broad smile. 'It's such a relief to be out of there!' He giggled as he stretched his neck. 'Balthazar Najar, genie genius at your service!'

Jamie shook his head. Was he seeing things? The boy didn't look like any of the genies he'd seen on TV or in films or read about in books. He was

much too young. Genies were supposed to be old and beardy and covered in wrinkles but this one couldn't have been more than sixteen. His pantaloons were torn and scruffy and loose threads hung from his waistcoat like little red worms.

'Y-y-you're not a genie,' stammered Jamie. 'You can't be! Genies don't exist and anyway, you don't look like one!'

'I *am* a genie,' huffed Balthazar pointing at himself. 'Pantaloons, waistcoat, pointy ears – genie!'

Jamie looked at the boy's ears. They were indeed very pointy.

'You could just have got that lot at a joke shop,' said Jamie.

Balthazar scowled. 'I can grant wishes too! Try me if you don't believe me!'

'What?' gasped Jamie.

'Come on!' Balthazar said. 'You released me from the teapot so you get three wishes. What'll they be?'

Jamie laughed. This was ridiculous! The whole thing was obviously some sort of birthday joke thought up by Dad and Gran. He bet that as soon as he started making wishes they'd burst in with a camera and shout, 'Surprise!'

Jamie looked the boy up and down

and smiled. He supposed he'd better play along. He had to admit it was an impressive trick with the smoke and everything – they'd obviously gone to an awful lot of trouble.

'So,' said Jamie with a mischievous smile, 'I can wish for anything at all and you'll grant it?'

Balthazar nodded. Then his eyes grew wide. 'Except frogs,' he spluttered. 'Don't wish for frogs!'

Jamie arched an eyebrow. 'Because you can't grant that wish?'

'No!' snorted Balthazar. 'Because frogs are all slimey and yucky and yurgh! I just don't like them.' Balthazar shuddered and stuck out his tongue.

'OK!' said Jamie, trying not to laugh. 'No frogs.'

Jamie searched his room for inspiration and when he saw his new poster, he knew exactly what he wanted to wish for. Not that it could come true of course. 'I wish I was a Formula One racing driver.'

'Easy peasy, lemon squeezy – nothing's hard if you're a genie!' sang Balthazar clapping his hands in delight. 'Your wish is my command!'

The genie closed his eyes and took a deep breath.

He seemed to be sucking all of the air out of the room. Jamie shook his head with a wry smile. What a performance!

Suddenly, Balthazar's eyes popped open and he blew a gust of air at Jamie that seemed to sparkle and shine. Jamie began to feel dizzy. He closed his eyes, just for a second, and when he opened them he found himself in the cockpit of a Formula One racing car, zooming around the track.

Jamie screamed in panic as he grabbed the steering wheel. The noise was terrific. The engine squealed like a jet plane and the steering wheel juddered in his hands.

'What's going on?' yelled Jamie over the screech of the tyres, trying not to sound scared.

A miniature Balthazar appeared on the dashboard in a flash of light.

'Don't shout,' said Balthazar, grinning. 'You'll fog up your crash helmet! You're a Formula One driver of course, just as you wished.'

'You really *are* a genie?' gasped Jamie. 'But I thought —'

A car whistled past them on the track. Instinctively, Jamie swerved to dodge it.

'Focus on driving!' Balthazar told him, and then grinned again. 'Try not to hit anything. This isn't like bumper cars. Just relax and enjoy yourself. I'll see you after the race.'

'*Relax?!*' screamed Jamie. 'I don't even know how to drive!'

But it was too late. Balthazar clicked his fingers and disappeared in a puff of smoke.

Jamie looked at the dashboard. It was covered in strange switches and dials. He pushed a big red button, the engine revved and the car went even faster. Jamie tried to keep calm. He gripped the wheel and did his best to steer. He hadn't crashed yet, and, as he got used to his surroundings, he somehow seemed to know exactly what all the controls did. Maybe that was part of the genie's magic – he had wished to be a racing driver after all, and they knew what they were doing. Pushing down on a pedal with his foot, his car sped towards the blue car in front. He cut it close, but passed by on the inside and zoomed on towards the grandstand. He was almost beginning to enjoy himself!

His heart pounded with excitement as he quickly changed gears and pushed down on the accelerator. Soon he was in the lead, but only just. The other drivers were right on his tail and using every trick they knew to try and overtake him. Jamie zig-zagged left and right and kept them behind his car as he streaked around the track. Being a racing driver was every bit as thrilling as he had hoped! Before long Jamie saw the chequered flag up ahead. He gunned the car's engine and raced towards it. As he zoomed past in first place, the cheers from the crowd were deafening.

He screeched to a halt, clambered out of the car and marched towards the podium.

Jamie posed proudly as hundreds of cameras took pictures of him clutching a huge trophy and waving at the crowd. The camera bulbs flashed, dazzling him.

When his vision returned, he found that he was back in his bedroom, still holding the trophy, and waving at Balthazar, who was sitting on his bed, picking fluff from his belly button.

'So how was that?' Baltahzar asked. 'Top gear or the pits? The pits, geddit?!'

Jamie smiled. Balthazar may be bad at jokes but he was brilliant at granting wishes.

CHAPTER 3

Jamie stared at his reflection in the trophy, grinning happily. That had been an absolutely fantastic wish! As he told Bathazar all about it, he got the distinct impression that the genie enjoyed hearing about his adventure every bit as much as he had enjoyed experiencing it.

'That sounds like such fun,' said Balthazar when Jamie finished his story. 'I might have to try that myself one day.'

Balthazar gripped an imaginary steering wheel and zoomed around the bedroom making racing-car noises. '*Nyeeeeeeeer! Nyeeeeeeer!*' he shouted as he hurtled past the bookcase. Suddenly the excited genie swerved to avoid Jamie's trophy and skidded into the laundry basket and knocked it to the floor. 'Oh no!' He giggled as he screeched to a halt. 'Pants on the track! Pants on the track!'

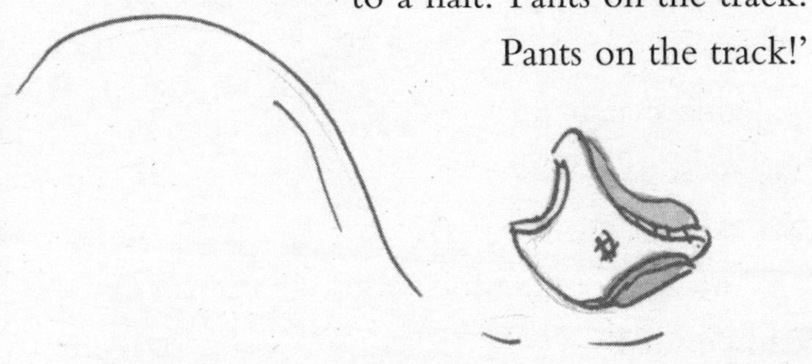

Jamie smiled. Whoever this genie was he liked him a lot, but his mind was bursting with questions. 'Why on earth were you in my teapot, Balthazar? I thought genies lived in lamps.'

Balthazar rolled his dark brown eyes as he bent down to pick up Jamie's stinky laundry. 'Genies don't *live* in lamps,' he explained, 'we live in towns and villages just like you, only up there.' Balthazar pointed at the ceiling.

'On the roof?' asked Jamie.

'No,' Balthazar said patiently, 'in the clouds.'

Balthazar held up one of Jamie's pongy socks and wrinkled his nose playfully. 'Aren't you a bit old for *Postman Pat* socks?'

Jamie snatched the sock away and chucked it into the basket.

'You were telling me about where you live,' he said pointedly.

'Oh yeah!' said Balthazar. 'Up in the clouds in towns and villages. We watch the human world from there and give out wishes when we see fit. Sometimes, when your wishes come true, it's because a genie has helped you out. We only get put in lamps as a punishment. Genies don't like being put in lamps. We don't like being trapped in the human world at all – we like to be free. When genies get put in a lamp, we have to stay there until someone releases us, by rubbing the lamp. And even when we are released, we can't go home until we've granted three wishes as a thank you. What does this do?'

Balthazar was fiddling with Jamie's *Star Wars* pod racer Lego model. It had taken him a whole month to build.

'Don't touch that!' shouted Jamie as Balthazar tugged on one of the pieces. It was too late. The pod racer fell to bits in his hands.

Jamie slapped his forehead. He had released a very clumsy genie.

'Oops,' said Balthazar defensively. '*That* clearly wasn't made properly.'

'Sit down and don't touch anything,' said Jamie. 'So why were you in a teapot and not in a lamp?'

'Ah!' said Balthazar. 'The first time a genie does something wrong they get banished to a lamp. The second time they do something wrong they get banished to a teapot. Then, if a genie does something wrong a third time, they are banished to a bottle at the bottom of the sea and they will probably never get out again.'

'So you're on your final warning,' said Jamie.

Balthazar nodded. He selected a book about insects from Jamie's shelf. The whole lot toppled onto the floor.

'I told you not to touch anything,' sighed Jamie.

'I didn't think you meant books as well,' said Balthazar. 'You should have said.'

Jamie shook his head. 'So what did you do to end up in the teapot?' he asked. 'Demolish a library?'

Balthazar clicked his fingers at Jamie. 'Good one! I can see we're going to get along! Actually, I broke the Genie Code,' explained Balthazar. 'There are five rules that all genies have to live by.' He counted them off on his fingers.

'Number one:
do not steal from another genie.

'Number two:
do not use your wishes for evil.

'Number three:
never back down from a genie challenge.

'Number four:
always obey your master when tied to
a lamp, teapot or bottle.

'And, most importantly of all, number five:
you must grant every wish your master asks.

'If you break any of those rules, you are punished. It's that last one that's the tricky one. I'm not brilliant at granting wishes.'

'You seemed pretty good at it to me,' said Jamie.

Balthazar beamed. 'That's nice of you to say but it's not always been that way. The first time I broke the Code was when I turned a man into a snowman because he wanted to be cool. Apparently, it wasn't what he wanted at all. Then the second time, a little girl asked to see a real dinosaur. I transformed her hamster into a T-Rex and it ate her mum. That got me into big trouble. It took a *lot* of genie magic to undo that wish. They're only allowed to be undone in the most dire of circumstances.'

Jamie felt sorry for Balthazar. He could tell that he never meant to upset anyone – he was clearly just a bit accident-prone.

'You've just been unlucky,' Jamie said. 'It wasn't really your fault at all. If people had been clearer about what they wished for, then nothing bad would ever have happened.'

Balthazar smiled. 'I like your thinking, Jamie, but genies are supposed to use common sense when it comes to wish granting. I get so excited that by the time I think about what might happen as a result of the wish, I've already granted it. Everyone thinks I do it on purpose, but I don't.'

Jamie patted Balthazar on the shoulder. 'Maybe you need a bit more practice,' he said.

'Shall we start with my second wish?!'

'Brilliant idea!' said Balthazar. 'Wish granting always cheers me up! What'll it be?'

Jamie thought hard. He'd had such a good first wish, he wanted his second one to be just as good.

Then he had an idea – there was one thing Jamie loved more than anything else in the world. 'I wish I had a bowl of never-ending ice cream,' he announced.

Balthazar nodded. 'Easy peasy, lemon squeezy – nothing's hard if you're a genie! Your wish is my command!'

Balthazar closed his eyes, inhaled deeply and then breathed out. The shimmering breeze enveloped Jamie once again, and once again he felt dizzy. When he opened his eyes he was holding a bowl piled high with delicious ice cream – vanilla, chocolate, strawberry, coconut, cherry and lots of other flavours Jamie didn't even recognise.

He sat on the bed and guzzled it down. As soon as the last spoonful was eaten the bowl magically refilled itself.

Balthazar was bouncing up and down on the bed in excitement. He really did love granting wishes!

Jamie picked up the spoon to start his second bowl when Balthazar bounced extra hard on his bottom. The spoon flew out of Jamie's hand,

through the air and splattered ice cream all over his curtains.

Jamie picked up the spoon and cleaned it on his T-shirt. 'You really need to be more careful,' he said.

'People are always telling me that,' agreed Balthazar. 'Especially my dad, Barakah. He said I could be the best genie in the world if I just listened properly.'

'So how do you grant wishes?' asked Jamie.

'You learn it at the Genie Academy,' said Balthazar, plucking a loose thread from his waistcoat which caused a button to ping off. 'It's all about breathing and blowing and a little bit of magic.'

'That sounds amazing. I wish I could go to Genie Academy and learn to be a genie,' said Jamie without thinking, as he ate another spoonful of chocolate ice cream.

He saw Balthazar's eyes light up like stars and he suddenly realised what he'd said.

'No! Stop! I didn't really mean it!'

But it was too late. Balthazar was blowing a deep, shimmering mist over him and Jamie felt the familiar dizzy feeling sweep over him once more.

CHAPTER 4

When Jamie opened his eyes, he found that he and Balthazar were standing in the middle of a market square, surrounded by shops and stalls – some tall and impressive, others ramshackle. But the strange thing was that every single one of them seemed to be made out of clouds. Even the ground was made out of clouds which wisped around Jamie's feet. Jamie took a tentative step, expecting to fall through at any moment, but the clouds held his weight and crunched beneath his feet rather like snow.

'Pretty cool, huh?' said Balthazar, grinning.

'W-w-where am I?' stammered Jamie.

'Lampville-upon-Cloud,' announced Balthazar, spreading his arms wide. Jamie ducked to avoid his genie fingers. 'Capital of the genie world. Right now you're standing in the Grand Bazaar.'

Jamie looked around. The Grand Bazaar was a riot of colour. Genies of different shapes and sizes were bustling around and haggling with market traders. Some wore red waistcoats like Balthazar, others wore green or blue or yellow. The Grand Bazaar was arranged around a square twice the size of Jamie's school playground. The town of Lampville-upon-Cloud stretched as far as the eye could see and Jamie gazed in amazement at the pristine white towers and spires that dotted the view all the way to the horizon.

'What am I doing here?' asked Jamie.

'You wished to go to the Academy and become a genie,' replied Balthazar.

'I didn't mean it!' protested Jamie. 'It was just something I said.'

'Here we go again!' huffed Balthazar. 'You humans are always saying things you don't seem to mean afterwards. Why say them in the first place?'

Jamie began to see why Balthazar got into so much trouble. Two genies at a nearby stall looked over at the arguing pair. When they saw Jamie their mouths dropped open. They pointed at his non-pointy ears and giggled. Jamie suddenly felt very out of place.

'This isn't the Academy though, is it? It's the middle of Lampville.'

Balthazar blushed. 'I thought we'd take the scenic route,' he muttered.

A small group of young genies had gathered in the doorway of a shop to stare at Jamie. Jamie stared back as one of them picked his nose.

'Everybody's looking at me!' hissed Jamie.

'We don't exactly get many humans up here,' Balthazar said with a shrug, 'and you have to admit your ears do look quite funny!'

'My ears!' spluttered Jamie. 'You're a fine one to talk, Mr Pointy!'

But Balthazar wasn't listening. 'In fact, you're probably the first human ever to come up here. Never mind! You're here now, so you may as well look around. The Bazaar is the heart of Lampville-upon-Cloud,' continued Balthazar in his best tour guide voice. 'It's where genies come to do their shopping, as you can see. You can buy all sorts of things here.' Balthazar pointed to a little shop in the corner of the square. 'That's Willie Eatme's place. He's the man to go to if you need a friendly snake.'

Jamie couldn't think of a time he'd ever need a friendly snake, but before he could say anything Balthazar was pointing at another shop.

'Then there's Ivana Waistcoat's clothes stall and that's Ivor Figburger's café. His figburgers are the best in Lampville. Fancy one?'

Jamie was too overwhelmed to answer.

'Maybe later,' said Balthazar. 'Then you've got Justin Time's clock shop and of course Mustapha Carpet's for all your flying carpet needs.'

'Did you just say *flying* carpets?' gasped Jamie.

'Oh yes,' said Balthazar. 'You've a lot to learn about genies, you know, Jamie.'

Balthazar put his hand on his hips and savoured the view. 'It's good to be back. Beats being stuck in a dusty old teapot, I can tell you! Anyway, we'd better get you to the Academy.'

'Actually, Balthazar,' said Jamie, 'I should probably be heading home.'

Balthazar arched an eyebrow. 'You made a wish to go to the Academy, Jamie, and become a genie. I have to grant it.'

'But I never really meant it!' said Jamie.

'It's too late,' insisted Balthazar. 'I've started granting your wish. If it has to be undone, or if I don't grant your wish fully, I'll be banished by the Genie Congress and this time it'll be a bottle at the bottom of the sea.' He stared intently at Jamie. 'I've never liked fish – they smell funny.'

'Then I'll make another wish,' said Jamie, closing his eyes. 'I wish I was back home.'

Balthazar shook his head. 'You've used up all your wishes, Jamie. You only get three.'

All the colour drained from Jamie's face. He was stuck there.

'There's no need to look like that,' said Balthazar.

'The Academy's great! Wish granting, basket weaving, killer snakes —'

'Killer snakes!' said Jamie.

Balthazar stopped short.

'Forget that last bit,' he said grabbing Jamie and whisking him down a small alley. The snakes very rarely kill. They might give you a nasty bite but they're only being friendly!'

'You're not making me feel any better,' said Jamie.

'It's a bit of a walk to the Academy,' said Balthazar, ignoring what Jamie had said and turning left at a ticking cloud clock. 'I'm between carpets at the moment, and that last wish really took it out of me. We'll just have to walk. If we hurry, we'll be there by nightfall.'

As Jamie and Balthazar made their way down twisty streets and across magnificent squares, the clouds under their feet crunched and squelched. Jamie couldn't help but be impressed.

'Are all the buildings in Lampville made out of clouds?' he asked.

Balthazar nodded. 'Of course. They're light and airy, can be twisted into any shape and there's loads of them about. They're like magic building blocks for genies.'

'But why don't we fall straight through them?' asked Jamie.

'This is an old, old world, Jamie. Lampville-upon-Cloud has been here so long that the clouds have set. They don't get blown into all sorts of shapes any more. They are what they are. Take that there.' Balthazar pointed to a majestic-looking building on the far side of a park. 'That's Cloud Hall. It's over a thousand years old – it smells like it too!' Balthazar wrinkled his nose. 'It's where the Genie Congress meet when there's something important to discuss. And here,' Balthazar pointed, 'is Lampville Jail.'

Jamie looked up at the forbidding grey building. It was the only building they'd passed that hadn't been fluffy and white.

'It's made out of storm clouds,' explained Balthazar. 'It's where we keep all the evil genies – the ones who grant bad wishes.'

Jamie shuddered. He hoped he'd never have to visit a place like that.

'Chop, chop, dawdle-drawers!' said Balthazar, picking up the pace. 'We have to skedaddle if we want to get to the Academy before lights out.'

They walked for what felt like hours across the cloudscape. Balthazar could obviously tell Jamie wasn't completely happy about being taken to the Academy and tried to cheer him up.

'What do clouds wear beneath their trousers?' he asked.

'I don't know,' said Jamie, genuinely puzzled.

'Thunderwear!' boomed Balthazar. 'They wear *thunder*wear! Geddit?'

Jamie couldn't help but laugh and soon Balthazar was telling him every joke he could think of. Most of them were about clouds. Jamie's favourite was, 'What do you call a sheep with no legs? A cloud!'

When Balthazar had run out of jokes, he kept Jamie entertained by telling him about some of the times his wish granting had gone wrong. He'd once made a bus loop the loop – making five old ladies lose their false teeth, and another time he'd even managed to invent a vampire duck.

By the time they reached the wrought iron gates of the Genie Academy, Jamie's belly was aching from laughing so hard. He found himself really liking Balthazar. He was a kind and funny genie who seemed to genuinely care about the people whose wishes he granted – even if the wishes did tend to go wrong.

'This is the Academy,' announced Balthazar, doing a little mouth trumpet fanfare, and pointing to the top of the gates. Carved across their top were the words, *Live Lightly and Shine Brightly*. 'It's the genie motto,' he explained. 'Genies are supposed to be light and airy in all that they do and shine brightly on others when granting wishes.'

'Like fairies?' suggested Jamie.

Balthazar fixed him with a fierce glare. 'We do not use the F-word in Lampville, Jamie!' he snapped.

He reached for a large golden bell rope that hung from the gatepost. 'The secret to this,' he explained, 'is to give it a good hard tug.' Balthazar yanked the rope sharply and it came away in his hands. 'Oops!'

There was a flash of bright light and a puff of

smoke as a genie in a red peaked cap and long coat appeared in front of them. His face was buried in a clipboard. 'Yes?' barked the doorman without looking up.

Balthazar hid the rope behind his back. 'Hello, Barir,' Balthazar said. 'I'm back!'

The doorman dropped his clipboard in surprise. 'Oh no!' he spluttered. 'Not you!'

Balthazar grinned. 'I've bought a friend.'

Jamie waved at the startled doorman.

The doorman stepped back in shock. 'It can't be. A h-h-human?' he stammered. 'At the Academy?! Just look at his horrible curvy ears! Oh dear, oh dear, oh dear! Methuzular! Come quick!' Then the doorman disappeared in a puff of smoke, as quickly as he'd arrived.

'Who's Methuzular?' asked Jamie.

'The headmaster,' said Balthazar. 'Me and him, we go waaaaay back!'

Suddenly there was another puff of smoke and a fierce-looking genie appeared at their side. This genie wore a golden robe, and a pair of bushy eyebrows clung to his forehead like two grey caterpillars. His eyes grew dark when he saw Balthazar standing in front of him.

'You!' he growled, looking the genie up and down. 'What are you doing here? I thought you'd been banished!'

Balthazar gave him a weak smile and pointed in Jamie's direction. 'He set me free,' he explained.

The fierce genie wheeled around and stared at Jamie in absolute rage. 'So this is your fault!' he bellowed.

Jamie closed his eyes and trembled. He really wished he could be back home, but he knew he was right out of wishes.

CHAPTER 5

The genie advanced on Balthazar. His fists were clenched and his eyes were blazing.

'What are you doing bringing a human to the *Genie* Academy?' He shouted so loudly that Jamie thought they could probably hear it as far away as the Grand Bazaar.

'M-M-Methuzular,' stammered Balthazar. 'I can explain!'

Methuzular silenced Balthazar with a stare. 'As

headmaster of the Genie Academy I should be sending you to the Genie Congress for this.'

'It's not his fault,' said Jamie quietly.

Methuzular wasn't listening. 'They'll lock you in Lampville Jail for a thousand years at least, and then you'll be begging to be banished!'

Jamie cleared his throat and tugged at the angry genie's golden robes. 'It's not his fault,' he said again, louder this time. 'It's mine. I wished to go to the Genie Academy. It's my fault.'

Methuzular considered the boy for a moment. He looked at him so closely that Jamie felt he was looking deep inside him. Jamie trembled.

A look passed across the genie's face that was hard to read. Was it surprise? Anger? Confusion? Jamie decided it was probably all of those things.

Then Methuzular turned to Balthazar. 'You were my worst pupil ever, Balthazar. How a genie as brilliant as your father ever produced you, I'll never know! In your five years at the Academy you managed to blow up the dining room, destroy your own dormitory and turn our caretaker Mr Clampfinger into a banjo.'

'The old meanie deserved it,' said Balthazar without thinking.

'And now, you bring a human to the gates of my Academy!'

'I had no choice,' said Balthazar standing his ground. 'Jamie freed me from the teapot. He was my master and he wished to come here. I have to grant him his wish. If I don't, I'll be breaking the Genie Code and be banished for the final time.'

'Which might have been no bad thing considering your track record,' said Methuzular.

'There's nothing in the Code that says humans can't come here,' said Balthazar sulkily.

'We didn't think anyone would be stupid enough to bring them!' snorted Methuzular.

Balthazar looked at the ground. 'Please, Methuzular,' he said quietly, 'what could I do? He wished to be a genie. I have to grant his wish. When it's done, I can rejoin my clan and you need never see me again.'

Methuzular raised his eyebrows. 'Believe me, Balthazar, that is a very pleasing thought.' He let out a weary sigh. 'You were only trying your best, I suppose. The human put you in a very tricky position. So, it all comes down to one question.' Methuzular adjusted his golden robes and pantaloons and turned to Jamie. 'Do you really want to be a genie?'

Jamie hesitated for a moment. He just wanted to go home. But then Balthazar would fail in his wish-granting, and be banished forever. Jamie bit his lip. He *had* made the wish, after all. He couldn't let Balthazar suffer for it – his new friend had only been doing what he thought right.

'Yes,' said Jamie with a nod. 'I really want to be a genie.'

Balthazar smiled in relief.

'And you promise to work hard?' continued Methuzular.

Jamie nodded again.

'Very well,' sighed Methuzular. 'I will let you into the Academy for one term only. If you pass the first exam, you will be considered a genie. The wish will have been granted, and Balthazar will be free to rejoin his clan.'

Jamie's eyes nearly popped out of his head. 'Did you say *term*?' he spluttered. 'I can't stay a term! I've got to be in school tomorrow!

And what about my parents? They'll be worried sick!'

Methuzular waved Jamie's concerns away as if he were swatting a fly. 'Up here time moves much faster than down there. A term up here is but a night down there. Your parents won't even notice you're gone!'

Jamie still wasn't sure – it sounded like a very long time to him.

'You are free to go home at any time,' said Methuzular, 'but if you do, Balthazar will have failed to grant a wish that he has attempted, breaking Rule Five of the Genie Code. He will be banished to a bottle at the bottom of the sea. It's up to you.'

Jamie looked at Balthazar. His dark brown eyes pleaded with Jamie.

It didn't seem to Jamie like he had much of a choice. 'OK,' he said quietly. 'I'll stay.'

CHAPTER 6

'It's going to be hard for you,' said Methuzular bluntly. 'You've already missed a couple of weeks of this term, and you're a human – well . . .'

Methuzular's words trailed off as he caught the young boy's eye. He looked at Jamie carefully, then he shook his head as if dismissing an annoying thought.

'Let's get you to a dorm,' he said quickly, pushing open the gates. 'You'll be joining Sifir class in the morning so I'll take you to Sifir boys' room.'

As Methuzular led Jamie through the gates of the Genie Academy, Balthazar called after him, 'What about me, sir?'

Methuzular turned and looked at him. 'Now that is a difficult question, Balthazar,' he said. 'You've been released from your teapot so you can't go back there, but you haven't successfully granted this wish yet, so rejoining your clan is out of the question.' Methuzular considered this for a moment. 'We always need help looking after the grounds and school. The clouds can get a bit wild.'

He clicked his fingers and a grubby genie in a pair of green overalls appeared at the gates.

Balthazar's face fell.

'You remember Balthazar, don't you, Mr Clampfinger?' Methuzalar smiled. 'I believe he once turned you into a banjo.'

Jamie gave Balthazar a little wave, then followed Methuzular into the imposing castle towering up in front of them.

Methuzular guided Jamie down a maze of corridors to a tower at the far end of the Academy.

'We're going up here,' he announced as they began to climb the narrow spiral staircase.

Jamie did his best to keep up, clinging tightly to the thick piece of rope that snaked its way up the wall. After a minute of steady climbing, Methuzular stopped at a doorway. Jamie could hear the noise of excited chatter coming from inside.

'The boys are in here,' said Methuzular, opening the door.

When the young genies saw their headmaster standing in their dorm the chatter stopped immediately. They all looked about the same age as Jamie but wore brightly coloured tops of yellow, blue, green and red.

'Your class has a new member!' announced Methuzular. 'Make sure he feels welcome. It's late now, but in the morning I want one of you to take him to the uniform store, and generally look after him. Can I have a volunteer?'

A pleasant-looking genie with blond hair and blue eyes raised a hand.

'Thank you, Adeel. I will leave Jamie in your capable hands.'

Methuzular ushered Jamie into the dormitory and then closed the door as he left.

For a moment there was silence as the boys examined the human intruder.

Then Adeel hopped off his bed and grabbed Jamie's arm. 'Don't mind them,' he said. 'It's just that we've never seen a human before, except in pictures. Did Methuzular say your name was Jamie?'

Jamie nodded.

'You humans have funny names. I'm Adeel by the way. Adeel Maloof. There's a bed next to mine that's free.'

As they walked towards it, Jamie counted fifteen genie boys. They were sitting on beds that were lined down either side of the dormitory. Some had been playing cards, others dominoes and a couple had been reading. But now they were all staring at Jamie.

As they neared the empty bed at the back of the room, a boy with thick black hair and dark brown eyes leapt down from his bed and barred their way. The boy glared at Jamie.

'He really is a human – look at his disgusting ears!' he spat, prodding Jamie in the chest with a bony finger. 'What are you doing in the Genie Academy?'

'Balthazar Najar brought me here,' said Jamie quietly.

A murmur of excited chatter rippled through the room.

'Balthazar Najar is back?' gasped the black-haired genie.

'I released him and for one of my wishes I asked to come to the Genie Academy and become a genie. If I don't, Balthazar will have failed to grant my wish and he'll be banished to a bottle at the bottom of the sea.'

'Best place for him,' sneered the dark-haired genie. 'We'll see what we can do to make you give up. We could start by getting you a bed in Alim tower. That would get you scurrying back home.'

The black-haired genie pointed out of the window to a scary tumbledown tower on the far side of the castle grounds. A shiver went down Jamie's spine.

'Alim Tower is the headmaster's old quarters,' whispered Adeel. 'Nobody goes there any more. It's supposed to be haunted.'

'M-M-Methuzular said I could stay here,' stammered Jamie.

'M-M-Methuzular said I could stay here!' mocked the nasty genie. 'But Methuzular isn't here now, is he? What do you think, Harb? Shall we show our guest to his new quarters?'

A large genie nodded, punched his fist and laughed.

'Stop it, Dabir!' Adeel snapped. 'You too, Harb! We're supposed make Jamie feel welcome.'

'I *am* making him feel welcome,' said Dabir as he moved away. 'Not,' he added under his breath, but everyone could hear.

'And the rest of you can go back to what you were doing too,' said Adeel. 'How would you like to be stared at like that on your first day?'

The other genies mumbled their apologies and headed back to their games and books.

'Thanks,' said Jamie.

Adeel grinned. 'Don't worry about Dabir. He

thinks he's better than everybody else just because he's a Ganim.'

'What's a Ganim?' asked Jamie.

'You really do have a lot to learn, don't you?' said Adeel, nodding to the empty bed. 'Sit down and I'll fill you in.'

Jamie sat on the bottom bed and Adeel sat on the bed opposite.

'The Ganims are one of the four great genie clans,' he began. 'There are the Ganims, the Najars, the Maloofs and the Kassabs. I'm a Maloof,' announced Adeel proudly. 'You can tell because I wear a yellow top. The genies in each clan wear a different colour. That way you can tell which clan they belong to. The Maloofs wear yellow, the Najars wear red, the Ganims blue and the Kassabs green.'

Jamie nodded as he lay back on the bed, looking round at all the boys in their different colours, but he could barely keep his eyes open. He'd had a long day at school, a birthday party and been magicked to another world – no wonder he was tired.

'You've missed supper,' said Adeel, seeing that Jamie was finding it all a lot to take in. 'But I can magic you up a figburger, if you'd like a snack?'

Jamie stifled a yawn and shook his head. He was too tired to be hungry.

'There are some pyjamas under your pillow and you can get changed in there.' Adeel nodded to a small room opposite their beds.

A curtain hung across the doorway like a department store changing room. Jamie changed into his silk pyjamas there, hoping, as he pulled on his pyjama bottoms, that everything would make more sense in the morning. He climbed into his bed. It was like lying on a giant marshmallow.

He closed his eyes and was asleep before his head hit the pillow.

CHAPTER 7

The cloud bed was the comfiest bed Jamie had ever slept in. He only woke up because Adeel was shaking him gently. Sunlight was streaming through an arched stained-glass window at the far end of the dormitory and the room was full of genies preparing themselves for another day at the Academy.

'Wake up, sleepyhead!' said Adeel. 'And hurry up, too! You need to get a uniform before breakfast.'

A few minutes later, a still sleepy Jamie had changed back into his human clothes and was following Adeel down the spiral staircase.

'So you said Balthazar Najar brought you here?' called Adeel over his shoulder.

'Yes,' said Jamie with a nod. 'I wished to be a genie, sort of, and Balthazar granted it.'

Adeel shook his head. 'That's going to make things hard between you and Dabir.'

'Why?'

Adeel turned to face Jamie. 'Dabir's family hate Balthazar's family.'

'What happened?' asked Jamie.

'A long time ago Balthazar's father Barakah and Dabir's father Dakhil used to be the best of friends. They were the two brightest genies in the Academy and vowed to be friends forever. All was well until they both fell in love with the same genie. When she married Barakah, Dakhil grew insanely jealous and vowed revenge. He never spoke to Barakah again and promised to do all he could to make his and his family's life difficult. Dakhil has been true to his word and it seems like

Dabir is going to follow in his father's footsteps.'

Jamie shook his head. That was a sad story.

'That's enough history for today,' said Adeel, scurrying off down the corridor again.

Eventually they stopped at a bright blue door. The words *Uniform Store* were scrawled across the top in gold ink. Adeel pushed Jamie inside.

A plump little genie looked up from her knitting. '*What* are you wearing?' she spluttered, looking Jamie up and down with a distasteful eye. 'Don't worry! Aunty Fadiyah will soon have you looking beautiful!'

Adeel laughed and shook his head. 'I don't think we've got time for that. Let's settle for less weird!'

The genie bustled over to a rack of brightly coloured waistcoats. 'What clan are you?' asked Fadiyah.

Jamie shrugged. 'I don't think I have one.'

'He was bought here by Balthazar Najar,' explained Adeel. 'Maybe that makes him a Najar too.'

'Perfect!' Fadiyah smiled and selected a shirt, pantaloons and waistcoat from the rack. 'You can get changed in there!'

Fadiyah pointed to a curtain, nudged Jamie towards it and soon he was wearing a silky genie outfit with a bright red waistcoat.

'Just like a proper genie!' Adeel smiled. 'Hungry?'

Jamie nodded. 'I could eat a horse!'

'I don't think we're allowed to eat those,' said Adeel, tactfully. 'Would a bacon sandwich do you?'

Jamie licked his lips and let Adeel lead him to the dining hall where he guided him to a cloud table. The aroma of fresh bacon and sausage filled the air.

'Where do we get the food from?' he asked hungrily.

Adeel scooped up some cloud from the table, inhaled deeply and breathed out. His sparkling breath magically transformed the cloud into a toasted bacon sandwich. 'You eat whatever you wish for in the Genie Academy,' said Adeel, handing Jamie the sandwich. 'You'll learn all about it in cookery class.'

Jamie was seriously impressed. Adeel magicked himself a bacon sandwich too and the boys tucked in.

The dining hall was filled with boy and girl

genies of different shapes and sizes, all proudly wearing their clan colours.

'Genies are at the Academy for five years,' explained Adeel as they ate. 'We're in Sifir class, which is the first class. There's about thirty of us altogether. Next year we move up to Wahid class, and we end up in Khamsa. After that, you go back to your clan and start granting wishes for humans you want to help.' Adeel licked his fingers. 'Speaking of wish granting, that's our first lesson. We'd better get to class on time – it's Methuzular's and he doesn't like to be kept waiting.'

Jamie and Adeel quickly finished off their sandwiches and joined the throng of genies making their way to the classrooms. On their way, Jamie passed Balthazar who was wearing a pair of dirty overalls and mopping the floor. He leant on his mop and gave Jamie a cheery wave, before slipping over on the wet floor and wedging his foot in the bucket.

'No slacking!' barked Clampfinger, appearing at his shoulder.

Balthazar jumped and splashed water all over Clampfinger's shoes. Clampfinger growled and chased a clanking Balthazar down the corridor.

Adeel raised an eyebrow at Jamie, who shrugged in reply as they went on their way.

The classroom was full of genies. The boys he'd shared a dorm with the night before had been joined by some girl genies of the same age, all with their long hair tied back in scrunchies that matched the colour of their waistcoats.

Everyone turned to stare as Jamie and Adeel entered the room.

'Here he is!' sneered Dabir. 'Balthazar Najar's latest mistake.'

Jamie blushed as he took a seat next to Adeel.

Methuzular swished into the room and called the class to order. He was carrying a battered leather book studded with gold.

'That's the Book of Wishes,' whispered Adeel. 'All the wishes known to genies are listed in there.'

'Let's continue where we left off yesterday, shall we?' said Methuzular.

He opened the book and ran a finger down a page. 'Today we'll be looking at attribute wishes. Banika, perhaps you can remind us what an attribute wish is?'

A pretty girl genie dressed in red turned to face the class. 'An attribute wish is a "make me like" wish,' she said, smiling. 'Humans are very fond of them. They like to wish they can jump like a kangaroo or run like a greyhound . . .'

'Or be ugly like Jamie,' muttered Dabir under his breath, but loud enough for everyone to hear.

Banika ignored him. 'That's when you use an attribute wish.'

Banika sat back down and Adeel whispered in Jamie's ear. 'There are lots of different types of wish. Good genies know how to grant them all. Transformation wishes, transportation wishes, manipulation wishes, creation wishes . . . They're all in Methuzular's book.'

Methuzular overheard him and smiled at the class. 'That's right, Adeel, they are.' He turned to Jamie. 'What do you know about wish granting?'

Jamie shrugged his shoulders. 'I know it's something to do with breathing in and blowing out.'

Dabir let out a snort and shook his head.

'That's part of it,' said Methuzular, 'but there's more to it than that. In order to grant a wish, you have to imagine it coming true with all your heart. You have to *will* it into being. You have to clear your mind of everything else and concentrate on that wish as if it were the only thing in the world that mattered. You breathe in to clear your thoughts, to focus your mind on the wish that must be granted. Then you breathe out with the certainty that it will come true.'

Methuzular smiled again. 'You must take your mind to a place where magic can happen and believe that it will. Experienced genies do that automatically, but learner genies often need a little help in finding that magic place in their mind. The wishes in my book are like little poems, I suppose. You breathe in, recite the poem in your head, and that transports your mind to the place it needs to be. The more you practise, the quicker the poem takes you there, until one day you no longer need the poem at all.' Methuzular let out a satisfied sigh. 'Magic!'

Jamie was spellbound by the wise genie's words.

'Of course,' warned Methuzular, 'I am the only person allowed to read from the Book of Wishes. It is a very powerful thing and could cause trouble in the wrong hands.'

Jamie nodded. He could see why Methuzular kept the book close to him.

The old genie turned back to his class. 'Today we're going to look at the poem that leads your mind to that special place where magic can happen and attribute wishes can be granted.'

The rest of the morning, Jamie and the class tried taking their minds to that special place. The genies practised on themselves and slowly, but surely, wishes were granted. Adeel wished to be as strong as an ox and was soon balancing three desks on his back. Dabir wished for more arms than an octopus and was busy writing in nine different exercise books with nine different hands. Only Jamie was struggling. He'd tried very hard to fly like a bird, but he ended up feeling more like a tit than a falcon.

'Keep practising, Jamie,' instructed Methuzular handing Jamie a notebook. 'Make notes about what works and what doesn't in this. Eventually you'll find your way.'

Jamie took the book.

'Put your name on the front so that you don't get it mixed up with someone else's.'

Jamie wrote *Jamie Quinn* in bold letters on the front of the book.

Methuzular looked at him. 'You don't think of yourself as a Najar, I see.'

Jamie shook his head. 'I'm not sure I would unless I actually pass the exam to be a genie,' he said sadly.

Methuzular looked at him kindly. 'It's going to be more difficult for you than the others because you're a human, and you haven't been brought up among genies but, if you work hard, I'm confident you'll get there in the end.'

Jamie wasn't so sure. He'd found the lesson very difficult to get his head round and hadn't formed a single wish. Maybe he just wasn't cut out for wish granting.

Through the window he saw Balthazar sweeping the corridor. Jamie shuddered when he remembered what would happen to his friend if he didn't become a genie. He gritted his teeth, closed his eyes and tried again.

CHAPTER 8

After a figburger lunch magicked by Adeel, it was time for afternoon class. Unlike Jamie's normal school, the Genie Academy had two long classes each day, one after breakfast and one after lunch.

Pausing under a strange portrait of an imposing-looking genie, Adeel took out his timetable. 'Tomorrow we've got history and cookery, on Wednesday we've got gym and geography and on Thursday we study the Genie

Code. We use Fridays to practise everything we've learnt that week.'

Jamie was glad to see some subjects he recognised among the strange genie lessons he knew he would struggle with.

'We're off to genie skills class now,' announced Adeel.

'What are genie skills?' asked Jamie.

'Flying, apparition, shrinking, Earth-gazing . . .' said Adeel. 'All the skills genies need in order to do their job properly.'

Genie skills were taught by a kind-looking genie called Farah.

'I've heard all about you,' she said with a warm smile as Jamie entered. 'I see you've become a Najar. Good for you!' Farah winked and pointed to her red top. 'As you can see, I'm a Najar too.'

Jamie smiled. He was glad to be in the same clan as someone as nice as Farah.

'Today I am going to introduce you to the Portal of Dreams,' announced Farah with a flourish.

A murmur of excitement rippled through the class as Farah wheeled out a large golden frame into the centre of the room. Whatever was in the frame was hidden behind a black cloth covered with silver moons and stars.

'Many of you will have heard of the Portal of Dreams,' began Farah, 'but few of you will have seen one until now.'

Farah whipped off the cloth with a flick of her wrist and the whole class gasped as one. The portal was the most beautiful thing Jamie had ever seen. It was a screen, taller than Farah, and on it was a mass of swirling cloud. As Jamie watched, it seemed to shimmer and sparkle in the light.

'But what does it actually do?' he asked, his voice filled with wonder.

'Among other things, the portal is a genie's window onto the human world,' said Farah, waving her hands in front of the portal like a mystic dancer.

The familiar shape of planet Earth appeared through the clouds. 'Genies observe the world through the portal and grant wishes for those who deserve them. We watch your world very carefully, Jamie.'

Once again Farah waved her hands in front of the portal and the image on the screen changed. Jamie gasped. They were looking at his street. It was the middle of the night and the moon was high in the sky. The familiar faulty street lamp opposite his house flickered in the darkness.

As he watched, the image in the portal paused

outside his own front door. 'But you can't watch everybody all the time,' said Jamie. 'The world's too big.'

'That's where the clans come in,' she explained. 'Each genie clan is responsible for granting wishes in a particular part of the world. The Maloofs look after Africa, the Ganims Asia and the Pacific, the Kassabs America and the Najars Europe. Each family in that clan has their own portal. They are given an area to keep an eye on and grant wishes when they see fit.

'Children aren't allowed into a room with a portal inside until they've been to the Academy – it stops accidents. Once a baby genie accidentally crept through a portal and was found peering at the Queen in Buckingham Palace!'

'There are so many different languages in the world,' said Jamie. 'How do you understand what people are saying?'

'A good question, Jamie,' said Farah. 'The portal also acts as a translation device. No matter what language is used in the country you are observing, the portal will translate it into the language you understand best.'

Jamie watched as Farah manipulated the image on the screen. It zoomed up towards the sky, stopping briefly to peer through Jamie's bedroom window. He felt a pang of homesickness when he saw his clothes and toys scattered across the floor. His old life seemed very far away.

The image on the portal took off into the clouds and the other genies gasped and chattered in excitement. This was a day they had long been waiting for.

Farah held up a hand for silence. 'Now who wants a go?' she asked.

Every hand in the classroom shot up. One by one, the genies took turns exploring the human world with the portal. The portal was like a giant interactive TV screen. You controlled it with your hands like playing a high-tech video game. The right hand controlled left and right and up and down while the left hand controlled forward and back. It took a lot of practice to get it right. Farah told the genies to use slow, fluid movements rather than quick jerky ones. When Jamie had his go he panicked. Before he knew it the portal image was hurtling off towards the stars. Farah quickly guided him back to Earth and, taking his hands in hers, showed him the right way to use the controls. Before long Jamie was starting to control the portal like a true genie, waving his hands in the air like a slow-motion ninja. Maybe playing all those video games had paid off after all!

By the end of the lesson, Jamie had a huge smile on his face. He'd seen the pyramids of Egypt, the Taj Mahal in India and Big Ben in London. It was like the best TV programme in the world – and everything he saw was real.

After dinner, Adeel showed Jamie how to play dominoes and after a couple of games and chatting to some of the other boys it was time for bed.

As Jamie changed into his pyjamas, his head swam with everything he had learnt that day. He may only have missed two weeks, but the other children had been preparing all their lives for the Academy. He felt like he'd never catch up.

Adeel was reading when Jamie got back to his bed. Jamie clambered in between the soft sheets.

'Did you enjoy your first day?' asked Adeel.

'Not really,' sighed Jamie. 'I didn't grant a single wish and I nearly crashed the portal.'

Adeel giggled. 'Don't be so hard on yourself! You'll get there in the end.'

'I don't think I'm cut out to be a genie,' said Jamie closing his eyes and settling down to sleep.

'Go home, then,' boomed an angry voice.

Jamie opened his eyes. Dabir was looming over him.

'The sooner you leave, the sooner Balthazar is banished for not granting your wish! I can't wait to see the back of the blundering nincompoop!'

Jamie glared at Dabir. 'Balthazar is my friend,' he said crossly.

'More fool you,' sneered Dabir. 'That genie's a

joke. My dad's the head of the Genie Congress and he's been trying to get him banished for years. His mistakes give all genies a bad name. Give up, go home and get him sent away for good. You'll be doing us all a big favour.'

Jamie leapt to his feet and grabbed Dabir by his top. 'Take that back!'

The other genies in the dorm had stopped what they were doing and were staring in Jamie's direction. Dabir smirked and shook his head. He inhaled deeply and blew a wish at Jamie.

Suddenly Jamie's fingertips were burning. He let go of the pyjama top and thrust his hand into a glass of water on his bedside table. His fingers fizzed and hissed as they cooled down.

'Don't mess with a genie, human,' snapped Dabir. 'I mastered the attribute wish, remember? How did it feel to have fingers like matchsticks?'

Adeel stood between Jamie and Dabir. 'That's enough, Dabir!' he barked.

Dabir grinned and backed away. 'You won't always have your friend around to stand up for you,' he called as he headed for his bed.

Jamie was fuming and it wasn't until well after Adeel had wished his hand better and the lights were out that he finally felt like sleeping.

Just as he was beginning to drop off, Jamie felt something slither across his leg. He sat up and kicked off the duvet. The thing slithered across his foot and Jamie screamed. He was being attacked! In an instant, the whole dormitory was awake. The thing slid across Jamie's belly and he jumped out of bed clattering into his bedside table. Suddenly the dorm was full of noise as the young genies struggled to find out what was going on.

The door flew open and Methuzular stood

framed in the doorway. The headmaster clicked his fingers and the room was instantly flooded with light.

'What is the meaning of this commotion?' he growled.

His eyes came to rest on Jamie. He was out of his bed and nervously prodding his sheets with a finger.

'There's something in my bed, sir!' he said.

'Well, it's not you, is it!' barked the angry headmaster as he marched towards Jamie's bed. He pulled back the covers and gasped. A long black snake hissed angrily at them both.

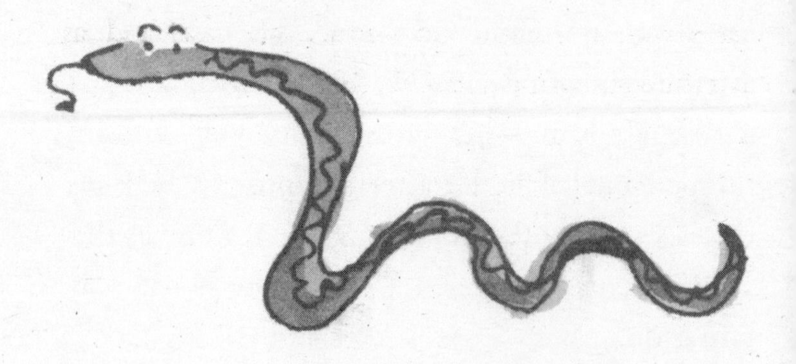

Dabir jumped off his bed and snatched the snake away. 'I'm so sorry, sir,' he said, his voice full of innocence. 'It's Fanghead. He must have escaped from his basket. I wonder how that could have happened?'

Jamie shot Dabir an angry look. He knew exactly how it had happened. It was clearly no accident that Dabir's snake had found its way to his bed.

'I'll lock him in the cellar if this happens again, Dabir,' warned Methuzlar, heading for the door.

When everyone had got back into bed, Jamie tried his best to settle down. As he pulled the covers around his ears, Dabir caught his eye and gave him a smirk. 'Go home,' he mouthed as Methuzular snapped off the lights.

CHAPTER 9

For the rest of the week Jamie did his best to keep out of Dabir's way and, with Adeel's help, he was soon getting the hang of life in the Academy.

Jamie enjoyed sleeping in a dorm. The pillow fights were great fun and he even managed to ignore Adeel's stinky feet – most of the time!

After the two long lessons each day there were all sorts of after-school clubs and activities to enjoy.

Jamie tried art club first because it sounded like something familiar from home, but when Adeel led him into the art studio Jamie realised he'd made a mistake. The room was full of genies painting pictures of a vase of flowers but none of them were actually holding their paintbrushes. As Jamie watched, they waggled their fingers to make the brushes dance magically across the canvas.

'Ready to give it a try?' asked Adeel with a grin.

Jamie wasn't sure, but Adeel was already setting up an easel and fetching him some paints.

'Ah! It's the human!' said Bashir, the art teacher, as he strode over to Jamie. He placed a stack of brushes next to him. 'Let's see what you can do. Start by concentrating on the brush.'

Jamie tried to imagine the brush flying into the air and covering the canvas with paint but nothing happened.

'Let me get you started,' offered Bashir. He took a calming breath, and focused on the brush. It leapt into the air, covered itself in blue paint and then floated towards the easel.

'Now you take over,' he urged.

Jamie looked at the hovering brush and willed it to make a mark on the empty canvas. The brush flew towards the canvas like a dart, made a jagged line on the page and then flew out of the window. Adeel stifled a laugh and Jamie felt his cheeks flush red.

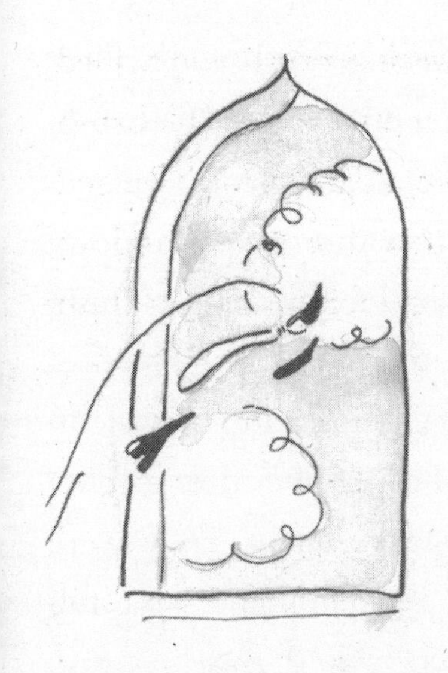

'A good first try,' said Bashir, leaning out of the window to see where his brush had gone. 'Your work shows real promise. Quite minimalist in its simplicity, with a touch of Picasso. You must come back next week and try again. If I've got any brushes left,' he added with a wink.

The next night, Jamie tried basketball. As they approached the gym, Jamie heard the familiar thumping sound of bouncing balls. He loved basketball, but when he saw how the genies played the game his jaw dropped. The baskets were ten metres off the ground and instead of jumping to score a point the genies flew around the court like birds. He spent the first game acting as referee from the safety of the ground, but for the second game Adeel gave him a piggyback and the two friends zoomed around the court together. Adeel did the flying and Jamie did the bouncing. They made a very good team and even managed to score a few points.

Every night that week held a new adventure and Jamie was introduced to the art of snake charming, learnt how to make the perfect figburger and even spent a night playing triangle in the Academy orchestra. Thankfully most of the other genies were nothing like Dabir. They were happy to have him in the Academy and were full of questions about his world and the toys and games he played with at home. Jamie realised that his way of life was just as strange to the genies as theirs was to him.

By the end of the week, Jamie was sure that there were no surprises left, but on Saturday morning Jamie learnt that Adeel had saved the best surprise until last.

CHAPTER 10

'Magic carpet racing!' spluttered Jamie over breakfast. 'You can*not* be serious!'

Adeel smiled. 'If you want to be a real genie you have to learn how to ride a magic carpet. So hurry up and finish your breakfast. Do you have your own flying carpet by the way?'

Jamie nearly choked on his sausage sandwich. 'Of course not!'

'Never mind,' said Adeel. 'I've got a spare.'

Jamie shook his head. He didn't see how that would make things any easier.

Adeel took Jamie out of the dining hall, through the front entrance and down a narrow path that led around the back of the Academy, past the laundry and between two cloud bushes.

The grounds of the Academy stretched into the far distance. Ornate fountains and beautiful statues of famous historical genies were dotted around smooth white lawns which were also filled with strange-looking cloud trees. At the far end of the gardens, spooky tumbledown Alim Tower loomed high above them. Even on a bright sunny morning it gave Jamie the creeps. He could understand why everyone thought it was haunted.

Adeel pointed to a single-storey building beyond a low wall. 'That's where we're going,' he explained. 'It's the stables.'

'But I thought we were going magic carpet racing?' said Jamie, getting a little confused.

'We are,' said Adeel matter-of-factly. 'Carpets have to live somewhere, don't they?'

As they made their way through a gap in the wall, Jamie was greeted by a very peculiar sight. Five magic carpets were racing round about five metres above a twisting track. On each one sat a genie in a pair of goggles, holding on for dear life. Other magic carpets were being fussed over and patted by their genie owners as they waited for a turn. One genie was even making some repairs with a needle and thread. Jamie watched as a brightly coloured carpet zipped past high above his head.

'Wow!' he gasped.

The track was roughly circular in shape and was about three times the length of a football pitch. Enormous cloud fences and cloud hedges were scattered around the track and as the carpets approached, they leapt over them like racehorses. Jamie could see the white knuckles of the genie riders as they clutched the carpets' tassles like handlebars. Each rider was wearing a helmet which matched the colours of their clan.

'Every genie learns how to ride a magic carpet,' explained Adeel. 'We all have our own. When you magic a carpet to life you create a special bond between you and the carpet. It becomes your friend forever. You look after it and it looks after you. Not every carpet races like this though,' said Adeel. 'These are the fastest.'

A red carpet flew past. The rider's teeth were clenched and sweat was trickling down his forehead.

'Do genies ever fall off?' asked Jamie.

'Oh yes,' Adeel told him. 'There have been some terrible accidents, but it's perfectly safe if you're sensible. Besides, Threadbare is one of the best all-round carpets in the whole Academy.'

'Threadbare?' said Jamie.

Adeel winked and, through the open stable door, a yellow magic carpet with a zebra stitched across its back reared up and zoomed towards him, smothering him in a big clothy cuddle.

'I think he's pleased to see me!' said Adeel giving him a pat. 'I don't ride him much any more.

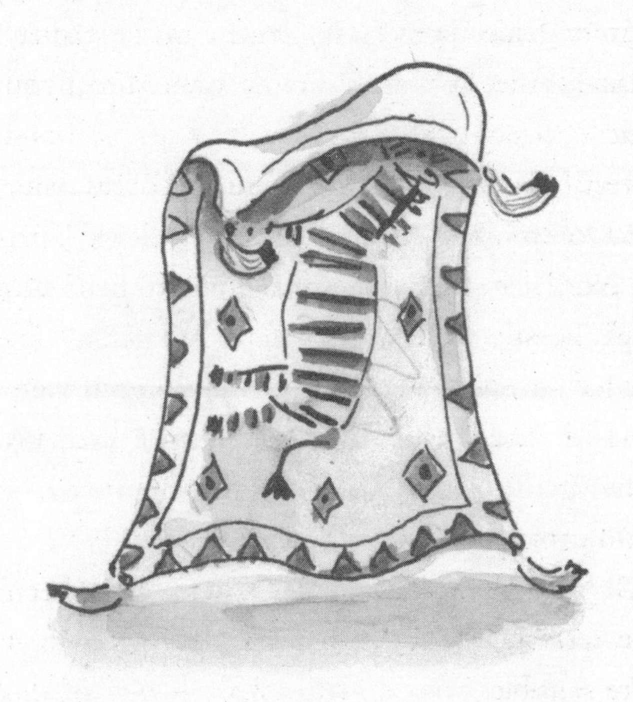

Since I got better at magic, I was allowed to magic myself a new carpet for my last birthday.' Adeel pointed to a sleek golden carpet in the next stall. 'Sunray,' he said proudly.

Adeel turned back to Threadbare and tickled his tassles. 'Threadbare will be good for you to learn on. You'll be nice to my new friend, won't you, boy?'

Threadbare reared up and turned towards Jamie.

Jamie backed away. As lovely as Threadbare seemed to be, he wasn't sure he wanted to fly on him.

'But he's yours,' said Jamie quickly. 'I'll watch.'

Adeel shook his head with a wry smile. 'Don't be such a scaredy cat. If you're going to become a proper genie, you have to start acting like one. Besides Threadbare could do with the exercise!'

Adeel took a pair of goggles from a shelf and threw them to Jamie. Jamie pulled them over his eyes and warily approached the carpet. He held out a hand and gave Threadbare a stroke. Like an over-eager puppy, Threadbare nuzzled Jamie's neck with his tassels.

'See?' said Adeel. 'He likes you.'

Jamie grinned. He had to admit there was something very cute about Threadbare. Together he and Adeel led the carpet out to the racetrack. Other carpets and their riders were zooming around it like giant buzzing flies. Jamie watched them zipping past and shook his head. He wasn't ready to fly. Even Formula One wasn't as scary as this!

'Don't worry,' Adeel said with a smile. 'We won't be doing that today. Let's just get you started. We can try out some basic moves in the paddock.'

Adeel led Jamie and Threadbare towards a large flat piece of cloud next to the racetrack. 'Up you pop!' said Adeel to Jamie, patting Threadbare's back.

The carpet lowered itself so that it was hovering just above the ground and Jamie tentatively put his left foot onto the silky cloth. He expected to fall straight off again, but to his amazement the carpet held his weight. With a smile, he lifted his other foot onboard and soon he was kneeling on the carpet.

'Grab his two front tassels like handlebars,' instructed Adeel. 'That's how you steer him.'

Jamie did as he was told and Adeel laughed. 'You're a natural!'

'A natural what?' sneered a voice from behind them. 'Wally?'

Dabir had appeared at their side in the paddock. He was leading his own magic carpet towards the racetrack. 'If ever you want to ride a proper magic carpet,' he said, 'I can lend you Viper.' Dabir gave his carpet a slap. 'Be careful though – he bites!'

Dabir's carpet reared up and lunged for Threadbare. Jamie held on tight as Threadbare dodged out of the way. Threadbare bucked and wobbled and Jamie struggled to stay on board. Dabir laughed.

'I think I'll get off now,' said Jamie quietly.

'Rubbish!' snorted Dabir. 'You haven't even had a race yet!'

Dabir stretched out a hand and yanked one of Threadbare's tassels. Before he knew what was happening, Jamie was racing out of the paddock.

He screamed as they headed towards the cloud fence that separated the paddock from the track. Jamie closed his eyes as Threadbare jumped the fence and zoomed onto the racetrack towards the first massive jump.

'Oops,' sneered Dabir, leading Viper back towards the stable. 'Watch out for carpet burns!'

Jamie clung on for dear life as Adeel shouted instructions to him. 'Pull on the left tassel! Now the right!'

Jamie did what he was told but it was no use – Threadbare was obviously too shocked to listen. They whistled past a startled rider, knocking him and his carpet sideways. The first jump towered above them like a skyscraper. They'd never make it! Jamie held his breath and clutched the tassels, yanking them both as hard as he could. Suddenly Threadbare screeched to a halt and Jamie felt himself flying through the air.

He was tossed from the carpet like a rodeo rider and tumbled head over heels into the clouds.

The other racers brought their own carpets to a standstill as Adeel clambered onto the track and rushed towards Jamie.

'I don't think I'm made for magic carpet racing,' groaned Jamie as he pulled himself out of the clouds.

'Nonsense!' said Adeel, relieved to see that his friend was all right. 'That was the best triple somersault I've ever seen!'

As Jamie picked himself up and dusted himself down, Adeel's eyes hardened. 'We should report Dabir to Methuzular for that,' he hissed. 'You could have been hurt.'

Jamie shook his head. 'That would only make things worse. I don't want to go running to the headmaster every time Dabir does something nasty. I even wish Methuzalar didn't know about last night. I need to stand on my own two feet if I want the other genies to respect me. Besides, there was no harm done.'

'Not this time,' said Adeel quietly as they led Threadbare back to the stable.

★ ★ ★

Scary though his first attempt at magic carpet riding had been, Jamie was hooked. Over the next few weeks, he returned to the stable every evening to practise riding Threadbare. Every weekend he and Adeel would race each other in the paddock, Adeel on Sunray and Jamie on Threadbare. Soon Jamie and the magic carpet were moving together in perfect harmony. Jamie even managed to beat Adeel every now and then, although Adeel always insisted it was because he hadn't been concentrating.

As well as magic carpet racing, Jamie enjoyed the art class the more he practised, just as long as Bashir made sure all the windows were shut. Much to his amazement, Jamie also got better at cooking – or magicking food out of clouds as he liked to call it. He made the best ice cream in the school and, in return for sharing some with his new genie friends, they would magic him whatever food he wanted but couldn't quite manage to wish for himself yet.

But Jamie was still struggling with lessons. He still hadn't managed to grant a single proper wish.

Once a week, Balthazar would come to the dorm and Jamie would update him on his progress. It was never good news.

'How's my favourite curly-eared human?' asked Balthazar one evening. 'Genie genius yet?'

'Not really,' said Jamie with a weary sigh.

'You'll get there in the end,' said Balthazar with a nervous smile. 'Jamie the genie has such a nice ring to it!'

'Never gonna happen,' said Jamie sadly.

Balthazar gave him a reassuring squeeze. 'You'll grant a wish any day now, just you wait and see! If I can do it, anyone can!'

But as the first half of term drew to a close and the genies began to pack their bags for home, Jamie still hadn't granted any wishes at all.

CHAPTER 11

At half-term, all the parents of the genies arrived to take the pupils back to their clans for a one-week holiday. Jamie watched through a stained glass window as an elegant procession of proud-looking genies riding large magic carpets made their way towards the school.

Jamie sighed sadly as he saw all the young genies rush to meet their parents. It only made him miss his own mum and dad even more.

'You could always come and stay with me and my family,' Adeel had offered. 'I can show you round Cloudhaven.'

Jamie gave his friend a rueful smile. 'I'm not sure that's a good idea. The other genies have only just got used to me here. Imagine the fuss I'd cause in Cloudhaven. Besides, I really want to be with *my* family not somebody else's – though I'm sure your family are lovely!'

'Most of them are,' said Adeel with a grin. 'Apart from my little brother – he picks the bits out from between his toes and then eats them.'

Jamie wrinkled his nose and thought of Paulie. He knew all about little brothers.

Before the genies departed for their holiday, Methuzular held an assembly in the great hall to fill the parents in on the progress the Academy had made that half of term. For normal assemblies the genies sat in their classes, but for this one they sat with their parents and clans on long cloud benches. The hall was divided into vivid blocks of colour determined by the genies' clan. Jamie made his way up the aisle to the red corner. As he walked, he felt as if a thousand pairs of eyes were watching his every move. The pupils in the Academy may have got used to having a human in their midst, but for the parents it was a very shocking sight indeed.

Jamie smiled at a fat genie with a long black beard and squeezed past him to sit down. The fat genie tutted and shuffled to another part of the bench. Jamie sighed. He was never going to fit in.

Methuzular made a long speech about the work that had been done in the school and the records that had been broken on the magic carpet track. After awarding some prizes to the lucky genies who had granted the most impressive wishes that half of term, Methuzular dismissed them all.

Jamie made his way alone down the long corridor to the dorm. He was going to be by himself at the Academy until classes started again. As he passed the headmaster's office he heard raised voices. He was about to walk on when he heard his own name mentioned. Filled with curiosity, he hid behind a large statue of the school's founder and listened.

'I don't care if you *are* the headmaster!' growled a voice. 'The human must go. The Genie Congress won't stand for it!'

'There's more to Jamie Najar than meets the eye,' said Methuzular quietly. 'He's —'

'He's a human!' interrupted the angry voice. 'That's all that matters. When Dabir told me what was going on, I couldn't believe my ears! What are you playing at, Methuzular?'

'This is my school, Dakhil,' said Methuzular, his voice quiet and authoritative. 'I decide what goes on here, not the Congress. There's nothing in the Genie Code to say that a human can't attend the Academy. Besides, he's only here for a term, and I had to let him come – Balthazar Najar was granting his wish.'

The other genie snorted. 'That genie should have been banished for good years ago! As leader of the Genie Congress, I'll make sure the human is out of this Academy as soon as he puts one foot wrong and Balthazar Najar will finally be put somewhere he deserves to be – a bottle at the bottom of the sea!'

The door flew open and a tall genie in a blue waistcoat bounded out. Jamie could tell by the familiar dark hair and scowling face that he was Dabir's father. The genie strode past Jamie with his nostrils flaring.

Jamie pulled himself out from behind the statue and turned sadly towards the Safir dorm. He slumped onto his bed and gazed around the empty room. There was a knock and Jamie sat up as a familiar face peered around the door.

'Balthazar,' said Jamie, forcing a weak smile. 'What are you doing here? Don't you get a holiday too?'

Balthazar shook his head. 'I'm not allowed back to my clan until your wish is granted. It looks like we're both stuck here! Isn't that good news?' He scampered over and gave Jamie a hug. 'I've barely seen you all term, *and* I've got a new joke for you! What do you call a cloud that can't get up in the morning?' He paused, waiting for Jamie to respond. 'Fog! Geddit? Fog!' Balthazar said eventually.

Jamie didn't even crack a smile.

'Not even a chuckle! Things must be bad. What's wrong, Jamie?' asked Balthazar.

'Seeing everyone else with their parents has made me homesick,' he said sniffing. 'I just wish I could see my mum and dad too.'

Balthazar considered this for a moment. He could understand how Jamie felt. He hadn't seen his clan for a very long time. There was nothing he could do about that but maybe he could make things a little better for Jamie. 'Your wish is my command,' he said proudly.

Jamie shook his head. 'I'm all out of wishes, Balthazar. Don't you remember?'

Balthazar grinned. 'Who needs wishes when you can get in to every room in the school?' he announced, triumphantly producing a key from his waistcoat. 'Follow me!'

Balthazar explained that he'd been given a set of keys so that he could clean all the rooms after lessons.

They walked down the deserted main corridor, coming to a stop outside Farah's classroom. Balthazar put the key in the lock and let them in.

While Jamie wondered what he was up to, Balthazar marched over to where the school's Portal of Dreams lay hidden under its black cloth. With a wink, Balthazar whipped it away.

'We can use it to check in on your parents,' he said.

'Are we allowed?' gasped Jamie.

'I won't tell if you don't,' Balthazar said.

The Earth spun in the frame of the portal and Jamie began to manipulate the image. He slowly zoomed in on the planet and guided the image left and right and up and down.

Balthazar arched an eyebrow. 'Wow! You're a portal pro, Jamie!'

Soon the screen was showing his street and, with a flick of the wrist, Jamie made the portal zoom up to his mum and dad's bedroom window and then finally into the bedroom itself.

From the light of the street lamp, he saw that his parents were fast asleep. He listened to his dad's familiar snoring and smiled. Usually it was the most annoying sound in the world but right now it was the only thing Jamie wanted to hear. The red light of the alarm clock told Jamie that it was three o'clock in the morning. Methuzular was right: time was passing much slower back on Earth.

Jamie suddenly felt very homesick indeed. He'd give anything to *really* be standing in his mum and dad's bedroom, if only for a minute.

As if reading Jamie's mind, Balthazar took a step towards the portal. 'There is something else that this portal can do,' he said with a smile. 'You won't learn about it until later in the term, but I don't suppose there's any harm in giving you a bit of a head start, is there?'

Balthazar lifted his leg and put it through the portal. The portal shimmered like a soap bubble and Jamie gasped. 'It's one small step for genies, one giant leap for Jamie's kind!' He giggled. 'A portal is more than just a funky television set. It's a gateway between our world and yours. Coming?'

Balthazar stretched out a hand and Jamie grabbed hold as the genie pulled him towards the portal. As he passed through, Jamie felt a ticklish tingle in his tummy.

Then he was standing in his parents' room. Jamie soaked up the familiar atmosphere, and the smell that reminded him of home.

He turned to Balthazar, his eyes filled with happy tears. 'Thank you,' he said quietly.

'It's hard to be away from your clan,' sighed Balthazar. 'I'm just glad you can visit yours every now and then.'

After far too short a time, they had to return to the Academy. As Balthazar led him back towards the portal, Jamie stopped. He turned and looked back at his sleeping parents and felt a lump in his throat. He didn't want to leave, he wanted to run across the landing to the safety of his own bed. He may only have been away for a few hours in human time, but in genie time he'd been gone for weeks. He missed his friends, his school and his family.

Balthazar stood with one foot in Jamie's parents' room and one in the Academy.

'I know what you're thinking, Jamie,' he said quietly. 'You want to stay here, don't you?'

Jamie could see Farah's classroom through the

shimmering portal and even though it was just a footstep away, it seemed very, very far from home.

Balthazar smiled sadly. 'The truth is you don't have to come back. I'm not going to force you. The choice is yours.'

Jamie took one look at Balthazar's face and knew exactly what he had to do. Balthazar had acted like a true friend in bringing him home and in trusting him to come back again. If he stayed behind now he'd be letting Balthazar down and banishing him to a bottle at the bottom of the sea. That wasn't what friends did. He stretched out his hand to Balthazar and the genie took it.

Balthazar had done something very special for Jamie. He vowed to work as hard as he possibly could to become a genie himself so that Balthazar could get back to *his* clan too.

For the rest of the holiday, Jamie took advantage of the empty Academy to practise everything he had learnt so far. Methuzular, who never left his precious school, patiently guided Jamie through his lessons again and again. Jamie slowly learnt to find his way to the special magic place Methuzular was always talking about. It was like a switch being flicked in the back of his mind, a switch that he hadn't even realised was there but, once found, made magic happen.

By the time the genies returned from their holiday Jamie had something very special to show Adeel and his friends. They'd never believe what he could do!

CHAPTER 12

'That. Is. Amazing,' Adeel spluttered as he walked into the dorm. Jamie was hovering a few centimetres above his bed with a proud smile on his face.

'Who needs a magic carpet, eh?' said Jamie.

Adeel dumped his bag on the floor. 'You've been practising!'

Jamie nodded and floated into the middle of the room. 'I wished that I could float like a balloon,' he explained, as he floated slowly towards the ceiling. 'I've been having extra lessons over the holiday and it's starting to come together.'

Adeel laughed as Jamie did the breaststroke while floating in mid-air. 'I hope you found time to keep an eye on Threadbare while I was gone,' he said, unpacking a new waistcoat.

'Don't worry,' said Jamie, 'he's fine. I even took him over a couple of the jumps. I'm getting good at that too.'

Just then Dabir stalked into the room. He sneered when he saw what Jamie was up to. 'Oh look! Has the human finally learnt a magic trick?' he said.

Jamie let his wish drift away, and landed back on the ground. If there was one person he hadn't missed over half term it was Dabir.

'I've been practising,' said Jamie.

'One lousy attribute wish! Is that it?' scoffed Dabir.

'Why don't you just pack up and go home? I've been practising too! Wanna see? Why don't you smell like an elephant!'

Dabir inhaled deeply and blew a wish in Jamie's direction. Jamie felt his nose begin to tingle, then gasped in amazement as it stretched like plasticine. Soon it was scraping the floor like an elephant's trunk. A couple of the other genies stopped their unpacking and began to laugh.

'Stop it, Dabir,' shouted Adeel.

'I'm just getting started,' said Dabir, drawing breath again, and blew a second wish at Jamie.

Jamie advanced on the arrogant genie, ready to give him a piece of his mind, but instead of shouting he began to bark. Now the rest of the dorm were laughing too.

Adeel turned Jamie back to normal with a wish of his own. 'You know the Genie Code, Dabir,' he snapped. 'You're not supposed to use your wishes for evil!'

'That wasn't evil,' said Dabir, laughing. 'That was fun! Besides I was just getting started! You should have seen what I had in mind for "As tall as a giraffe"!'

Jamie lunged angrily at Dabir, but Adeel held him back. 'You can't win against him,' he hissed. 'You need more practice.'

Jamie slumped onto his bed and punched his pillow in frustration. If he couldn't beat Dabir, he decided he'd better keep as far away from him as possible during the rest of his time at the Academy.

For the next few weeks, things carried on as normal until the morning Jamie and Dabir were paired together in Farah's genie skills class.

'One between two, please,' she instructed, placing a golden lamp on the desk that Jamie was reluctantly sharing with Dabir. Dabir's usual partner Harb and Jamie's partner Adeel had both come down with a nasty cold that was making its way through the school that no wishing seemed to shift. The boys had been told to stay in their beds until they felt better. Neither Dabir nor Jamie were happy about having to work together.

'Today we start lamp practice!' announced Farah.

The genies groaned, but she silenced them with a hand. 'I know! I know! Nobody likes to think of themselves trapped inside a lamp. But while I hope that none of you ever end up in a lamp, it's best to be prepared.'

On the other side of the classroom, a nervous genie called Omer raised his hand. 'Will we really be stuck in this, miss?' he asked in horror, looking at the lamp in front of him.

'Don't worry,' said Farah. 'These are practice lamps. The proper lamps are up there.' Farah pointed to the shelf above Jamie's head.

'You don't get to use those until you are in Khamsa class. Spending a night in a real lamp is the final test to pass before you leave the Academy. A human wishes you out and you grant your first three proper wishes.'

Jamie looked at the two lamps. They seemed

identical to him.

'How do you tell the difference?' someone asked.

'They look the same on the outside,' said Farah, 'but the proper lamps are much more comfortable on the inside – after all, genies spend longer in them. And there are only two ways out of a proper lamp. The first is when a human summons you, either on purpose or by accident. The second is if you know the special wish hidden deep inside Methuzular's book. Of course, only he knows that, and he's not telling!'

The other genies laughed.

'Practice lamps will automatically release you after five minutes, summoned or not.'

Omer breathed a sigh of relief.

Farah explained that the best way to get into a lamp was to use an attribute wish. If the genies imagined themselves as small as fleas they would then be small enough to slide down the spout. She said that it would take a lot of concentration so the genies should try be as quiet as possible while the shrinking was taking place.

Jamie wasn't sure he was up to the challenge but luckily Dabir volunteered to go first into their lamp. Jamie watched as Dabir closed his eyes, breathed in deep and blew out the shrinking wish. His breath sparkled in the air and he shrunk to the size of a flea, tumbling down the spout of the lamp. Jamie looked around him and realised that every lamp had a tiny genie in it.

Jamie looked at the lamp. Dabir was trapped inside. It was the perfect opportunity to get his own back on the big bully now that he wasn't quite so big. He thought about pouring Dabir out through the spout and squashing him under his thumb, then shook his head. He didn't want to hurt him that badly. He could give the lamp a little shake – that wouldn't do much harm! Jamie smiled as he imagined Dabir being buffeted back and forth inside the lamp like he was on a giant rollercoaster. Jamie could even make him do a loop the loop or three! Jamie grinned at the thought, but of course he couldn't do anything – after all, he was going to have to go in the lamp once Dabir came out.

When five minutes had passed, the lamps spat out thick, coloured smoke, releasing the genies back into the classroom.

'That was a doddle,' grunted Dabir, turning to Jamie. 'Now it's your turn. Ready?'

Jamie tried to get his mind to the special place that he knew he had to find, but as the rest of the genies seemed to effortlessly shrink into their lamps, he found himself still standing in the classroom. Yet again he was the only one not to have completed the task. He began to panic.

'Calm down,' said Dabir. 'You'll have to relax if you want to grant the wish. Do you want me to help you?' Dabir smiled. 'I know we haven't been the best of friends, but maybe we should put that behind us and start again. What do you say?'

Dabir held out his hand. In a daze Jamie shook it. He didn't know why Dabir was suddenly being nice to him, but he was glad that he was. He suddenly felt guilty for even thinking of giving Dabir a rollercoaster ride. 'We've got to be quick,' hissed Dabir. 'I'll do the wishing for you, OK? You have to close your eyes,' he instructed.

Jamie was about to protest that he should be learning to do things on his own, but he didn't want to be the only genie that hadn't managed it. He didn't want to cheat, but he needed all the help he could get. He would make sure he practised later. He glanced around the room – everyone was absorbed in the task.

Jamie closed his eyes.

'Now wait a moment, I just have to get myself ready . . .' said Dabir, and Jamie heard him shuffling round.

Soon Jamie heard Dabir breathe in and blow a wish at him.

Jamie felt every part of his body begin to tingle. He opened his eyes to see his fingers shrinking to half their normal size. They became so small he thought he'd never be able to hold a fork again! Jamie watched, cross-eyed, as his nose disappeared into his face. His legs were shrinking and the desk began to rush towards him – except the desk wasn't rushing towards him, *he* was rushing towards *it*! When he was small enough, Dabir picked him up between a thumb and forefinger and popped him down the spout – rather roughly, Jamie thought.

'Down you go!' said Dabir, his voice sounding like a thunder crack to Jamie's tiny ears.

Jamie closed his eyes and slid down the spout as if it were a water flume at his local swimming pool. He landed with a thud and took a look around.

The lantern had purple walls, a purple ceiling and there was a soft purple armchair at one side and a soft purple bed at another. He was standing

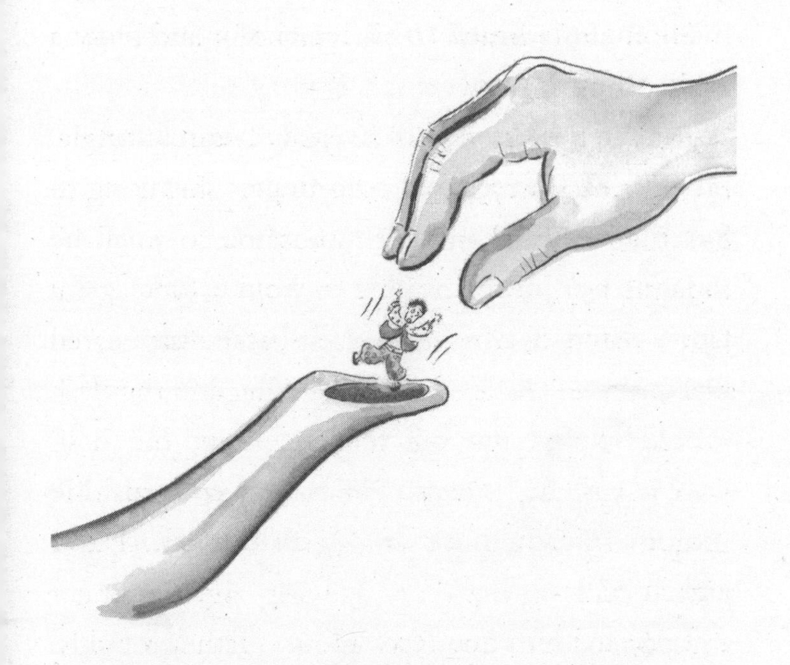

on a soft purple carpet that was covered in tiny sparkles. Jamie was pleasantly surprised – it was much more comfortable than he'd expected. If the practice lamps were like this, the real ones must be super luxurious. Jamie tried out the comfy chair, then laid back on the bed and waited for the five minutes to pass.

Outside he could hear the excited giggles of the other genies as they whooshed out of their lamps. After a while, he started to get restless – the five minutes seemed to pass very slowly. It was a good thing he'd accepted Dabir's offer of help, otherwise he'd have been even further behind the other genies. He stood impatiently and waited. Surely there wasn't long to go now?

Jamie was just beginning to wonder if he had a faulty lamp when he heard Farah talking to Dabir.

'Has Jamie come out yet?' she asked.

'Oh yes,' lied Dabir. 'He had to rush off. He promised he'd check in on Adeel before the afternoon lesson.'

Jamie heard Farah tut. 'He should have asked before leaving,' she said angrily.

It took Jamie a few seconds to realise what had happened. Dabir had tricked him – he must have swapped the practice lamp for a real one. Of course he should have guessed the moment he landed in the lamp. Why would a practice lamp have a bed in it? Why, oh why had he been stupid enough to trust Dabir?

He punched the wall in anger. He felt a cold bead of sweat trickle down his neck. The purple walls of the lamp seemed to be closing in on him and his heart began to thump. He scrambled at the wall trying to climb back towards the spout but his fingers slipped against the polished purple walls. He tried yelling and banging but there was no way anyone was going to be able to hear him. It was no use. How was he ever going to get out of the lamp? Jamie crumpled onto the floor in a defeated heap.

But he soon realised that feeling sorry for himself wasn't going to get him anywhere. The only way he was going to get out of the lamp was if he used his brain. He looked around for something that might help. Maybe he could use the bed to get to the spout or, even better, the lid! He slowly heaved the bed to the centre of the lamp and began to jump, using the bed like a purple trampoline. His mum would tell him off for doing this at home, but Jamie felt sure she'd understand why he was doing it now.

Little by little, Jamie bounced higher and higher. His outstretched fingertips touched the underside of the lid but try as he might he couldn't bounce high enough to knock it loose.

As he fell back onto the bed, exhausted, Jamie heard the bell ring for the end of class. The lamp began to move. Jamie clung to the bed and held on as best he could as the lamp swished and swayed. Then it stopped rocking and the lid flipped open. Jamie shielded his eyes against the light and looked up into the face of Dabir. Each of Dabir's teeth was bigger than Jamie's head and his grin looked like the terrifying sneer of a monster. Jamie felt like a trapped mouse waiting to be eaten by a ruthless cat.

'You should have left when you had the chance,' said Dabir. His voice boomed into Jamie's ears, as if coming from a thousand loudspeakers.

'Let me go!' yelled Jamie, his own voice sounding like a tiny squeak by comparison.

'Can't,' Dabir said smugly, giving the lamp a shake and knocking Jamie to the floor. 'Only a human can release you and, oh no – the only one around here is you!'

Jamie groaned. He'd forgotten that. 'Methuzular can help. Farah said he's got a releasing wish in his book.'

Dabir grinned down nastily. 'But, like everyone else, he'll think you've run away. Just like you said in your letter.'

'What letter?' hissed Jamie pulling himself back up.

Dabir waved a piece of paper at Jamie. 'This one.' Dabir blew into the lamp and his breath felt like a tornado, knocking Jamie onto the floor. Dabir's laughter bounced off the walls.

'When everyone hears that you've gone, Balthazar will have failed to grant his wish and my dad can get rid of him once and for all! That'll show Barakah Najar who's boss!' Dabir lifted a massive meaty finger and waggled it threateningly at Jamie. 'I could squash you right now, of course,'

he taunted, 'but where would be the fun in that? Humans keep genies in lamps. Why can't I keep a human in one?'

Dabir ignored Jamie's angry squeaks. 'You should be grateful that I'm letting you be my pet,' he continued. 'I'll keep you somewhere nice and safe so no one will ever find you.'

And with that, Dabir closed the lid. Jamie clambered onto the bed and clung on as the lamp began to move once again.

CHAPTER 13

The lamp rocked and swayed for what felt like hours. At first Jamie tried to work out where Dabir was taking him by listening out for familiar noises. He recognised the chatter of the genies as they passed the dining hall, heard the thud of the main entrance as it closed behind them and felt the lamp rock as Dabir took him down the front steps and out into the Academy grounds. After that, sounds became more difficult to place. All

Jamie could hear was the crunch of Dabir's footsteps on the cloud beneath them and the rush of the wind through the trees.

Then Jamie heard a door creak open and felt himself being jolted up a long flight of stairs, before finally they came to a stop. Dabir gave the lamp a shake. The purple floor rocked beneath Jamie like an earthquake.

'Wakey, wakey, Jamie!' said Dabir, flipping open the lid once more. 'Welcome to your new home!'

Jamie was furious. 'Let me go!' he yelled.

Dabir shook his head. 'I couldn't even if I wanted to. Only a human or Methuzular's special wish can get you out of here.'

Dabir smiled as all the colour drained from Jamie's face. 'Don't look so scared,' he said. 'You'll be nice and safe in Alim Tower.'

Jamie's heart sank as he remembered the creepy abandoned tower at the edge of the school grounds that he'd seen before. No one would ever find him now.

'Let's put you up here,' said Dabir, closing the lid and popping the lamp on a high shelf. 'That way you'll be out of harm's way. Now I must get back to lessons.'

Jamie sank onto the bed as he heard Dabir's footsteps walking away. There was no point in calling for help – Jamie's tiny body meant he only had a tiny voice. Besides, Alim Tower was deserted.

Tears welled up in his eyes. Dabir's note would make it look like he'd left, and so nobody would come looking for him. Balthazar would be banished to a bottle at the bottom of the sea for failing to grant his wish and everyone would think it was Jamie's fault. Neither of them would ever see their families again. He lay back on the bed, exhausted, and eventually fell asleep.

Sometime later, Jamie opened his eyes wide and sat up. Something had woken him. He had no idea if it was day or night, nor how long he'd been inside the lamp, but he'd heard a noise – he was sure of it. He held his breath and listened. Someone was coming up the steps. It must be Dabir returning to taunt him some more. But the footsteps sounded different. They were heavier than Dabir's and whoever it was seemed to be running. Jamie heard the door burst open.

'Hide! Hide! I've got to hide!' said a voice that Jamie recognised instantly. What was Balthazar doing there?

In the dusty tower room, Balthazar dragged a battered old chest away from the wall and crouched behind it. A thin film of sweat glistened on his forehead. He scanned the room for anything that he could cover himself with. Old carpets hung on the walls and faded portraits sat propped against broken chairs and tables. In desperation, he yanked a carpet down and draped it over his head. Balthazar prayed that no one would find him here. When it seemed that Jamie had run away, it meant that he'd failed to grant his wish. He was due to be banished for a third and final time by the Genie Congress. But he could only be banished if they knew where he was.

High on a shelf sat a gleaming golden lamp. Balthazar closed his eyes and groaned. He didn't need reminding of lamps and teapots and bottles.

Why had Jamie let him down? It seemed so unlike him.

Back in the lamp, Jamie was screaming for help as loudly as could – which wasn't very loud at all.

Balthazar looked up. He'd heard something.

What on earth could that be? For some reason it reminded him of Jamie. He was obviously hearing things.

In the lamp, Jamie's voice was hoarse from shouting. He knew Balthazar was there and he had to get his attention. Then he had an idea. He headed to the far corner of the lamp and ran towards the opposite side clattering into the metal wall with his shoulder.

Balthazar popped his head out from under the carpet again. What was that? Was somebody else in here? Had they found him already?

Jamie tried ramming the lamp again and Balthazar saw it wobbling and stood up to have a closer look. Jamie took one last run up and gave it everything he had. It was going to hurt, but there was nothing else he could do.

Balthazar dived out of the way as the lamp flew from the shelf, whistled past his ear and clattered onto the floor. What was going on? He ran over to the lamp and picked it up, flipping open the lid. Balthazar felt a shiver run down his spine as he stared at the familiar purple interior of the lamp.

He'd spent so long inside a lamp that he never wanted to see the colour purple again!

Lying on the floor face down in the carpet was a tiny little figure. As Balthazar looked closer he could see from his top that he was a Najar.

'Are you all right in there?' called Balthazar. 'That was quite a fall!'

Jamie picked himself up and gazed up at the open lid. He was feeling very dizzy.

'Jamie!' spluttered Balthazar. In his excitement he dropped the lamp. As he fumbled to catch it, Jamie was spun like a sock in a washing machine. When the lamp was safely on the floor Jamie felt dizzier than ever.

'Thank goodness you found me!' he groaned. 'But what are you doing here?'

'What am *I* doing here?' said Balthazar. 'What are *you* doing here and what's happened to your voice? You sound like an angry grasshopper!'

'I'll tell you all about what happened to me in a minute,' said Jamie. 'Tell your side first.'

'I'm in hiding,' explained Balthazar. 'Everyone thinks you've run away. They want to banish me.

So I thought I'd hide in Alim Tower until I thought of a way to escape. What about you?'

In his squeaky little voice, Jamie told Balthazar all about what Dabir had done.

'Those Ganims,' he spat when Jamie finished. 'You just can't trust them.'

'Well, now you're here, get me out!' said Jamie.

Balthazar bit his lip. 'I don't think I can, Jamie. This is a real lamp, isn't it? The only way out is if a human summons you or you know the spell to get yourself out. Only Methuzular knows that spell, and of course he won't tell anyone – he doesn't want banished genies setting themselves free. It's in the Book of Wishes and that's kept locked in his office . . .'

Balthazar's voice trailed off. When Jamie looked up, he saw him staring into the distance.

'What are you thinking?' said Jamie, irritated.

Balthazar held up his cleaner's set of keys. 'I have an idea,' he said smiling.

Jamie shook his head. 'No! You can't, Balthazar. If you go back to the Academy to fetch the book and they catch you, they'll banish you for certain.

We need to go to Methuzular together and explain what's happened.'

'I wouldn't even get the chance to open my mouth,' said Balthazar, shaking his head. 'He'd just see me holding a lamp and send me to the Genie Congress there and then. I've never seen him this angry, not even when I launched the tool shed into space.' Balthazar fell silent. 'I could go and get the book tonight while everyone's asleep,' he said eventually.

'You might still get caught,' said Jamie.

'What have I got to lose? If we don't get you out of the lamp I'm as good as banished anyway.'

Jamie nodded. Balthazar had a point.

'You're my friend, Jamie,' continued Balthazar. 'We're in this together. If I can get you out of the lamp then we might have a chance of explaining everything to Methuzular.'

Jamie agreed. It was their only hope.

Night came quickly and Balthazar watched from the window as the lights in the castle were flicked off one by one.

'Wish me luck,' he said quietly as the final light went dark. 'I might need it.'

Jamie wanted to stretch out his arms and give his genie friend a reassuring hug. Instead he squeaked, 'Good luck!'

Jamie strained his ears, listening to Balthazar's footsteps as he crept from the room and scurried down the stairs. When he could no longer hear them, he settled back in his purple bed, waiting impatiently for Balthazar to return.

The moon was high in the sky when Jamie heard the door at the foot of the stairs creak open. Immediately he was wide awake and alert. He listened to the footsteps tread softly up the stairs. Were they Balthazar's or Dabir's?

The door opened and Jamie breathed a sigh of relief as Balthazar called into the room, 'Hi honey, I'm home!'

Jamie grinned as Balthazar's beaming face loomed into view high above him. He waved the Book of Wishes at Jamie. 'Ready for a bedtime story?'

Jamie nodded eagerly.

'It was a close call,' said Balthazar. 'I nearly got caught three times, but thanks to my top secret moves I managed to dodge out of the way.'

Balthazar waved his hands in the air like a big red ninja and grinned.

'We'd better get a move on!' urged Jamie. 'If Methuzular finds out his book is missing not even your ninja moves will get us out of trouble.'

Balthazar quickly flicked through the pages, his eyes growing wide as he studied secret wish after secret wish.

'Oh my goodness,' he said, whistling through his teeth. 'I've got so much to learn!'

'Just hurry up and get to the right page,' said Jamie.

Balthazar leafed through the wishes. Finally he looked up. 'There are lots of different rhymes for escaping from a lamp, a teapot and a bottle.' He paused. 'I wonder . . .'

Jamie could see that Balthazar was tempted to look up how to save himself in case he was banished to the bottle after all.

'Balthazar!' called Jamie. 'There's no time! Hurry!'

'Don't worry,' he said quietly. 'Here's the one for escaping a lamp – but it's going to be tough.'

Jamie's heart sank. 'How tough?'

Balthazar shook his head. He had a grim look in his eye. 'Tougher than a boxer who's just got out of tough school and is feeling very tough.'

'I don't stand a chance.' Jamie sighed. 'I'm rubbish at wish granting.'

Balthazar peered down at his friend. 'Don't worry, Jamie! I'll help!'

Jamie huffed angrily. 'That would make it worse! You're the whole reason I'm in this mess! If it weren't for you I wouldn't even be in the Academy!'

Balthazar sat down on the floor next to the lamp and sniffed back a tear. 'You're right,' he admitted. 'Maybe I should hand myself in and be banished. A bottle at the bottom of the sea might

not be that bad. I might meet a friendly shark. It's probably what I deserve.'

Jamie felt bad. He had taken his anger out on Balthazar, but he wasn't to blame for everything that had happened. Most of the fault lay with Dabir.

The thought of Dabir, with his mean face, made Jamie angry. He couldn't let that slimeball beat them! He needed Balthazar's help.

'I'm sorry, Balthazar,' said Jamie. 'I didn't mean to be cruel. You're the kindest, funniest and best genie

I know. I'd be honoured if you would help me wish my way out of this lamp. And I know that, however difficult the wish, you'll be able to help me.'

Balthazar wiped his eyes with his sleeve and peeked in at Jamie. 'You mean it?' A massive tear rolled down Balthazar's nose and into the lamp. Jamie dived out of the way to avoid a thorough soaking.

'Of course I mean it!' Jamie said. 'Now get me out of here before I drown!'

Balthazar read the magic poem to Jamie.

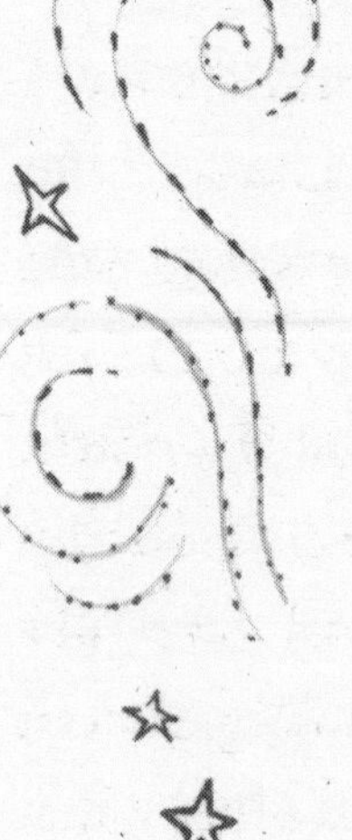

'When the world is nothing
but a lamp
to me,
And all of my body
longs to be free.
I just close my eyes,
and believe
I'm a bird.
Flying through the skies,
with the power
of my word.'

Jamie closed his eyes and repeated the rhyme over and over again in his head, waiting to feel that special click that meant the secret part of his mind was open. He breathed in and focused as if his life depended on it, which it probably did. Jamie blew out. Nothing happened.

'Try again!' encouraged Balthazar. 'You were close that time – I could tell.'

He listened to Balthazar's kind words and suddenly he really believed that he could make the wish come true. Jamie felt the air fill his lungs once more and his mind relax. As if in a dream, he saw himself flying across the sky like a bird. He was there. He knew it was time.

Jamie blew out, seeing his breath sparkle. He felt a tingle in his tummy. It was working!

The lamp filled with bright blue smoke and suddenly Jamie was flying up the spout. He felt like a champagne cork being shot out of a bottle. As he flew back out of the spout, one by one his fingers grew back to their normal size like balloons being inflated. He felt his nose grow out of his face like Pinocchio. Had it always been that big? Just as he was about to land in a heap on the floor, his legs shot out from his hips and saved him. He stretched his arms high above his head, felt his back click and turned to face Balthazar. He rushed towards the genie, arms outstretched. One of the best things about being back to normal was that he could give his friend a hug.

'Thank you, Balthazar! Thank you so much! You have no idea how great it feels to be out of that lamp and back to my right size.'

'Believe me, I do,' Balthazar said with a wink. 'Now we have to get the book back before Methuzular realises it's gone!'

Balthazar ran for the door, and Jamie followed close. But as Balthazar reached for the knob, the door suddenly flew open with a force that sent it flying from its hinges. Standing there, eyes filled with fury, was Methuzular.

CHAPTER 14

Methuzular snatched the Book of Wishes from Balthazar's hands and clutched it to his chest. He glared at the trembling genie and shook his head in disgust. 'How *dare* you?' he spat. 'Did you really think this book would be so easy to steal?'

Balthazar tried to speak but no words would come.

'This book is protected by magic,' growled Methuzular. 'I knew it had been taken and I knew exactly where it had been taken to. You have committed a terrible crime, Balthazar Najar.' The headmaster's words were filled with venom. 'You have stolen this book and broken the Genie Code for the last time. I have already spoken to the

Congress. They are expecting us there this evening. They will banish you on the spot.'

Balthazar tried to speak up. 'But Methuzular —'

Methuzular silenced him with an icy stare. 'I've had enough of your "buts", Balthazar. I listened when you blew up the dining hall, I listened when you turned Mr Clampfinger into a banjo, I even listened when you arrived at my gates with a human! But now you have run out of excuses.'

Jamie came out from behind Balthazar. 'Maybe I can explain,' he said.

'Jamie!' he spluttered. 'We thought you'd left!'

'Dabir tricked me into a lamp. We were supposed to be practising but Dabir swapped the practice lamp for a real one then he left me here.'

Methuzular shook his head. 'Not even Dabir would do a thing like that.'

'He would and he did, Methuzular,' said Balthazar.

'But you left a note,' said Methuzular, and a scroll of paper appeared out of thin air beside him. 'Look.'

Jamie snatched the note. 'It's a good copy, but

that's not my writing. Plus, he's signed it Jamie Najar. You know I don't consider myself a Najar yet. I might wear Najar colours but I'm not a proper Najar genie yet. I still sign my name Jamie Quinn, remember?'

Methuzular nodded slowly as he now remembered the discussion they'd had in his class all those weeks ago.

'But why would Dabir do something like that?' asked Methuzular.

'Dakhil Ganim hates my father and my family,' said Balthazar quietly. 'He vowed to do everything he could to punish my dad for marrying my mum. What better way to punish him than by getting his son banished to a bottle if Jamie failed to become a genie?'

'By making everyone think that I'd run away, he made everyone believe that Balthazar had failed,' explained Jamie.

'Even if all of this is true, Balthazar still stole my Book of Wishes. That is in itself a banishable offence,' Methuzalar said.

'He only borrowed it! And we wouldn't have

had to do that if Dabir hadn't tricked me. He could have stolen the book any time to look up how to save himself from the bottle at the bottom of the sea, but he didn't. He only took it to look up the wish that would save me.'

Methuzular locked at Balthazar with a new respect, but then shook his head. 'Be that as it may,' he said, 'the Congress still expect to see us in Cloud Hall in half an hour.'

'But they'll banish him for good!' pleaded Jamie. 'All my work will have been for nothing!'

In the corner, Balthazar's eyes quietly welled up with tears.

An idea flashed into Jamie's head. 'Tell the Congress that *I* stole your book, not Balthazar.'

Methuzular shook his head. 'I couldn't possibly do that, Jamie,' said the old genie.

'You could,' said Jamie, staring deep into Methuzular's eyes. 'The Congress know the book was taken, but they don't know for sure that it was Balthazar who took it. I'm not even a genie yet. Tell them that I wanted to practise, that I'm fed up being bottom of the class, that I thought if I borrowed the Book of Wishes – and that's all I was doing – then *maybe* I'd get better.'

Methuzular considered Jamie's pleas for a moment. He looked at Jamie with the same strange curiosity that Jamie had noticed before, when he first arrived at the Academy.

'You'll make a very good genie, Jamie,' he said, 'but I can't lie to the Congress.'

Jamie began to protest but Methuzular held up a finger for quiet. 'I will do my best to save Balthazar from banishment, but I can make no promises. The Congress make their own decisions.'

Jamie thought of Dakhil Ganim, leader of the Genie Congress and Dabir's father. If Balthazar's fate lay with him, he didn't stand a chance. As Methuzular, Balthazar and Jamie made their way on the stately school flying carpets towards Cloud Hall, Jamie had a very bad feeling in the pit of his stomach.

Cloud Hall was the impressive building Jamie had

passed on his first day in Lampville. It was covered in ornate swirls of golden cloud and imposing statues of important genies peered down on them from on high.

Methuzular led Jamie and Balthazar into the waiting hall where genies in flowing robes bustled in and out of lavishly decorated side rooms. Methuzular instructed Balthazar and Jamie to wait in two uncomfortable-looking chairs while he went to speak with the Congress.

'I will do my best to explain everything,' he reassured them as he disappeared through the large carved doors that led to the Congress chamber. 'And Balthazar,' called Methuzular, 'don't touch anything!'

From their place outside the chamber, Jamie and Balthazar listened silently to the raised voices of the debate. Jamie recognised Dabir's father's voice straightaway. He was speaking loudest of all. It was clear that Dakhil wanted to banish Balthazar and send Jamie home.

Methuzular explained that he had been hasty in calling the Congress, and that Balthazar had only borrowed the book. Dakhil snorted. That might be what Balthazar was saying now but he still took the book. Methuzular spoke earnestly to the Congress. He told them that Balthazar was foolish, that he had made a mistake, but he also had a kind heart and deserved one last chance. Dakhil shouted that Balthazar had been given too many last chances. Other voices joined the debate and soon Jamie had lost track of who was speaking when and whether they were on Balthazar's side or not. Eventually the talking stopped and the doors swung open. Methuzular walked slowly from the room and sat down with a heavy sigh.

'They are giving you a final chance,' he said quietly to Balthazar.

Jamie cheered and gave Balthazar a big hug.

'It's late,' announced Methuzular turning to Balthazar. 'Why don't you get the flying carpets ready to take us back to the Academy?'

Balthazar scampered eagerly from Cloud Hall and ran towards the Grand Bazaar. When he was gone, Methuzular turned to Jamie. 'It was a close vote, Jamie,' he explained. 'Dakhil was determined to see Balthazar banished and you sent home. I pointed out to Dakhil that if it turns out Dabir trapped you in a real lamp he was breaking some very serious rules himself and might find himself expelled from the Academy. Dakhil didn't like the idea of that and promised to take it easy on Balthazar if I in turn take it easy on Dabir.'

'Was that enough to convince the rest of the Congress?'

'Almost,' sighed Methuzular. 'I also put my reputation on the line. I promised that if Balthazar made another mistake, I would answer for it personally and resign as Headmaster of the Academy.'

Jamie gasped. 'You would do that for Balthazar?'

Methuzular smiled. 'By offering to take the blame, you were prepared to do the very same thing. Genies give to others. It's what we do, Jamie. You reminded me of that. I think I've been too harsh on Balthazar in the past. As the school motto says, we live lightly and we shine brightly.

Offering to take the blame for Balthazar shows that you understand that as much as the rest of us. And that makes you, in my eyes, a genie.'

'Balthazar is a good friend,' said Jamie. 'He risked getting caught and banished in order to get the book that would set me free. He took a risk to give a chance to someone else. I guess that makes him a good genie, too.'

Balthazar called to them from the archway. He had three flying carpets hovering by his shoulder. As they walked towards him, Methuzular leant close and whispered in Jamie's ear, 'Of course, it also helped when I told them what I knew the first time I saw you: you've got genie blood.'

Jamie stopped dead in his tracks. 'No, I haven't!' he said.

But Methuzular was already on a carpet and being whisked away into the night.

CHAPTER 15

Could he, Jamie Quinn, really have genie blood in him?

Jamie did his best to catch the headmaster up so that he could quiz him on what he had said but Methuzular was too fast and by the time they reached the Academy, he was nowhere in sight.

Jamie thought of asking Balthazar about it, but he didn't really know what Methuzular had meant. Jamie thought it best to keep it to himself for now. He said goodnight to Balthazar instead, and crept quietly to his bed.

He was woken the next morning after just a few hours sleep by yelps of surprise from all the other genies.

'How did you get here?' asked Dabir in disbelief.

Jamie glared at the dark-haired genie and then flashed him a cool smile. 'Sometimes friends are stronger than enemies,' he hissed.

Suddenly Methuzular appeared in the doorway. 'Dabir Ganim!' barked the headmaster. 'My office. Now! You have some explaining to do!'

Dabir hung his head in shame and sloped off towards Methuzular's office.

The other genies were shocked to see Jamie back in their dorm. They all thought he'd run away. Jamie explained what had happened. He told them about the forged note and Dabir's plan to keep him as a pet. The genies shook their heads in disappointment. They couldn't believe that Dabir was capable of such a thing.

'Methuzular will kick him out of the Academy for good,' said Adeel.

'No, he won't,' said Jamie. 'Balthazar stole the Book of Wishes to help set me free. In order to save Balthazar from banishment, Methuzular struck a deal with Dakhil. Dabir will be punished but not expelled.'

Adeel punched his pillow in frustration. It seemed to him that Dabir was getting away with it too easily.

But Dabir did not get off lightly. Methuzular put a bed out in Alim Tower where Dabir was to sleep alone as an example to the others.

He was able to attend lessons, but he was banned from any after-school club for the rest of the term. Instead, he had to do chores with Balthazar and Clampfinger. His first job had been to polish all the lamps in the school until they sparkled.

As the end of term approached, Jamie studied harder than ever. Balthazar helped him whenever he could and Adeel made sure they were always paired together in class so that he could explain the things Jamie didn't understand.

Methuzular's revelation in Cloud Hall still played on Jamie's mind but, despite his best efforts, he couldn't get the headmaster on his own to find out more. It was almost as if Methuzular regretted what he had said and was trying to avoid him. Instead, Jamie decided to focus on other things. When he wasn't studying, he passed every spare moment he had down at the stables with Threadbare and, after more falls than he could remember, he was riding the carpet like a real genie pro.

The dorm had been full of gossip about the final exam for weeks. Adeel told Jamie that his older brother had said that in the exam they would have to use the portal to grant a wish for a human in the real world.

Jamie gulped. He could barely manage to grant wishes for himself – he'd never managed a proper one for someone else. But Jamie knew that if he passed the test, he would be considered a genie and Balthazar would be free to rejoin his clan. If he failed, he could go home and continue his life as before, but Balthazar would be banished to a bottle at the bottom of the sea. Jamie found the responsibility daunting. There was more pressure on him than on anyone else and he wasn't sure he was up to the challenge.

The day of the final exam arrived. Methuzular met the Safir genies after breakfast, gave them a reassuring smile and led them to the school hall.

He clapped his hands and Farah appeared from a side door, wheeling the Portal of Dreams.

'This test will use every skill you've learnt at the

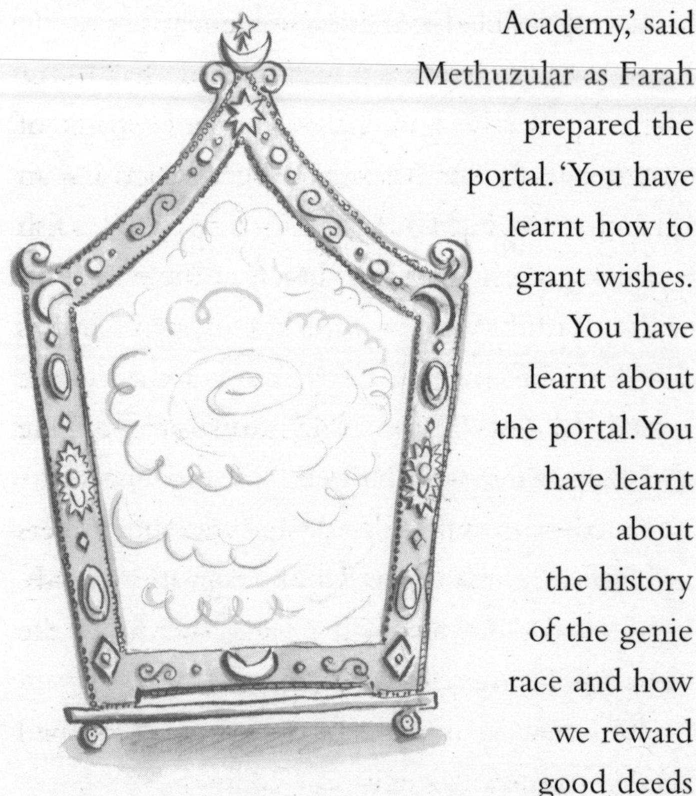

Academy,' said Methuzular as Farah prepared the portal. 'You have learnt how to grant wishes. You have learnt about the portal. You have learnt about the history of the genie race and how we reward good deeds with wishes. Today you must put all of that into practice and grant a wish for a human.'

The genies looked worried. In school they could grant wishes in safety, knowing that if anything went wrong, a teacher could put it right. It wasn't like that in the real world. They'd be on their own, granting wishes for other people and being responsible for the consequences.

Jamie had only just learnt how to do half of the wishes properly and he still made loads of mistakes. Only last week he'd been practising an attribute wish. He'd been trying to swim like a fish but had given himself fish fingers at the end of his hands instead. Making mistakes on himself was one thing, but making a mistake on someone else was very different. What if he hurt somebody? He could never live with himself.

Farah manipulated the portal with her fingers and planet Earth appeared through the clouds. With a twirl of her little finger she made the portal zoom in on Africa.

'We will do this clan by clan,' explained Methuzular, 'starting with the Maloofs.'

Adeel got to his feet and joined the seven other Maloof genies in front of the portal.

'Each genie must use the portal to find a suitable human and then grant their wish,' said Farah. 'Remember all that you have learnt and good luck!'

While the rest of the class looked on, Adeel

used the portal to find a human that needed his help. His search took him to the savannah where a young tribesman was in trouble. The sun was beating down on the sandy ground and strange birds circled high above the dried-out shrubs and trees that were dotted around. The tribesman was a goat herder and he and his goats were surrounded by hungry-looking hyenas. Their jaws were covered in drool and their teeth glinted in the sunlight. The tribesman shook his staff at them but the hyenas just growled at him and moved a little closer. Everyone could see that if Adeel didn't do something quickly then the tribesman's goats would be eaten. The tribesman's eyes were filled with fear.

Adeel manipulated the portal so that he was hidden from view and then stepped through onto the savannah. Jamie watched as he breathed in deeply and blew a sparkling wish towards the hyenas.

'He's using a transformation wish,' hissed Banika.

When the wish cleared, Jamie saw that Adeel

had transformed the hyenas into fluffy little pups.

One rushed towards the tribesman and began to nibble his toes playfully.

The tribesman rubbed his eyes. He couldn't believe what he was seeing. He scooped up the hyena puppy and tickled it under the chin. His goats were safe. Adeel stepped back through the portal and the image disappeared.

Back in the hall, the genies cheered. Adeel had done it! Jamie gave Adeel a thumbs-up and the proud genie grinned. Jamie was relieved too; Adeel was good at magic, so if he had failed, Jamie knew he wouldn't have stood a chance.

For the rest of the morning, Jamie watched as the Maloofs, the Kassabs and then the Ganims granted wishes for the people they watched over. Dabir was allowed to take the exam although no one cheered when he passed the test.

Jamie was amazed by the things his genie friends could do – whole houses were wished into being and worn out clothes were transformed into brand new ones. An old lady was transported to Australia to see her grandchildren and a farmer was given rain so that his crops would grow.

But eventually the Najars were called to the front and, with trembling legs, Jamie walked to the portal.

CHAPTER 16

All the other Najar genies went first, but soon there was no putting it off, and it was Jamie's turn.

Farah nudged him towards the portal. 'Last but not least, Jamie,' she said. 'Good luck.'

Jamie took his place in front of the screen and raised his arms, guiding the image to his hometown. He wanted to be on familiar ground for his test. The sun was just starting to rise and one or two early morning joggers were pounding the streets. Jamie realised, with concern, that it wouldn't be long now before his parents would be expecting him downstairs for breakfast. He had to go home soon.

As Jamie searched frantically for someone to help, Balthazar slipped into the back of the hall. He smiled nervously at Jamie and took a seat.

Jamie realised he mustn't get distracted – this test wasn't just about him becoming a genie, it was about saving Balthazar from banishment too. He had to concentrate.

He focused on the screen and zoomed up the high street. There must be someone who needed his help. Jamie flicked his wrist and spun the image on the portal past a thousand familiar sights: the park where he played football with his friends, the fast food café where Dad bought them secret Saturday burgers, the cinema where he'd watched so many fantastic films. It all seemed a lifetime away. He found it hard to believe that in human time he'd only been away a night.

He switched direction with a finger and spun the portal towards the town hall. As the image flew, Jamie spotted another jogger up ahead. Jamie sighed. What help could a jogger need? He turned the portal up a side street past the twenty-four hour supermarket. Maybe one of the shoppers had a wish he could grant. But the shop was empty so Jamie turned around and headed back the way he had come.

As Jamie moved the portal over the main road, he noticed that the jogger he'd seen by the railway line earlier was still there. Jamie manoeuvred the portal towards her. When he got closer, he saw that something was wrong – the jogger was tugging frantically at her leg and sweat was pouring from her brow. Jamie gasped when he realised that her foot was stuck between the rails of the level crossing.

Jamie knew in an instant that this was his chance. He zoomed the portal over to the large bin that sat outside the railway station and stepped through. He checked that nobody had seen and then crouched behind the bins to think.

The jogger was about the same age as Jamie's mum. Her trainer laces were undone but she was panicking so much that still she couldn't get her foot out of the shoe. She bent down and yanked at it but it wouldn't budge. She hit her leg in frustration and cried out loud.

Just then a warning siren sounded and the gates of the level crossing began to close. Jamie's heart leapt – there was a train coming!

Jamie could hear a rattle and hiss and spotted the lights of the train in the distance. The jogger seemed to freeze with terror as the train got closer and closer. Even if the driver managed to see the jogger, there was no way he could stop the train in time.

Jamie's mind began to race. What could he do that would help? And then he had an idea: he could do a transformation spell. He remembered the wish that took him to that special place where magic could happen, but he had to think fast to adapt it to this situation.

'Maloof yellow and Ganim blue
Transform this person
into something new,
Najar red and Kassab green,
Give her the smallest foot I've seen!'

Nothing happened.

Jamie cursed himself. He wasn't going to be able to do it. It had been hard enough back in the classroom but now it was a matter of life and death. Jamie knew he had to calm down. He had to empty his mind of all these thoughts and focus on one thing and one thing only: granting that wish. He had to clear space in his head and let the wish grow.

Jamie closed his eyes and breathed deeply. He tried to block out the panic of the jogger and the rumble of the train on the tracks. He imagined the jogger's foot shrinking as he repeated the rhyme again and again. As he got lost in the rhythm and the sound of the words, Jamie felt his mind shift. He felt the click and knew that the wish was ready. He inhaled deeply and blew it towards the jogger.

As he watched the sparkles envelop her, the world seemed to go into slow motion. The jogger looked down in astonishment as her foot began to shrink. When it was small enough, she yanked her leg clear of the track and jumped out of the way. But to Jamie's horror, she stumbled and fell, lying across the tracks.

The train was going to slice her in two!

Without hesitating, Jamie took a deep breath, closed his eyes and blew. He had no time to recite rhymes, he just imagined the jogger floating like a balloon.

The sparkles closed around the jogger and she began to rise. Her mouth opened in astonishment

as she soared up into the sky and hovered over the train.

Jamie watched the driver rub his eyes in disbelief as he zoomed under her. Once the train had passed, Jamie let his attribute wish disappear and the jogger floated gently back to earth. She picked herself up, checked her foot, which was normal-sized once more, and shook her head in amazement, gazing up into the sky in gratitude.

He'd done it! The wish to float like a balloon was the first wish he'd learnt how to grant back in the half-term holiday and he'd practised it every day since. It hadn't failed him now.

Jamie felt relief flood over him. The jogger was safe. He turned and saw the smiling faces of his classmates through the portal. As he stepped back into the Academy, his friends cheered and whooped.

'A double wish!' said Methuzular impressed. 'The mark of a true genie is someone who can think on the spot and grant wishes using instinct alone. You've managed that, Jamie. Well done! Double points!'

Jamie grinned.

'I believe that makes you a genie,' said Farah, ruffling Jamie's hair. 'And congratulations everyone – you've all passed!'

At the back of the hall Balthazar gave Jamie two thumbs-up and a silent round of applause as everyone crowded round to congratulate him. The only one who stayed away was Dabir. Jamie didn't mind. Dabir could sulk all he wanted to. Nothing was going to ruin the moment. He beamed from ear to ear. He'd done it. He was a proper genie!

CHAPTER 17

The hall was decorated in the colours of the four genie clans and banners hung from the ceiling. A stage had been erected at one end of the hall and Methuzular stood at a podium smiling proudly at the assembled genies. Adeel and Jamie huddled on a bench with the rest of their class, waiting excitedly for the ceremony to begin.

It was the last day of term, and those genies who had passed their exams were rewarded at a

grand ceremony in front of their parents and the rest of the school. Jamie's tummy was tingling with anticipation. He wasn't sure if he was more excited by the thought of being a proper genie or by the thought of finally going home. Since passing his exams, Jamie had realised how much fun being a genie was. Helping the woman when she was in trouble had felt wonderful. Jamie may have wished to learn to be a genie by accident, but now he realised it had actually been the best wish of all.

'Genies,' boomed Methuzular, calling the school to order. 'Let the ceremony begin.'

In a corner, the school orchestra piped up and began to play a rousing tune as the older genie classes stood to shake Methuzular's hand and receive their badge of honour. Soon it was the turn of the youngest class. Methuzular silenced the orchestra with a look and spoke to the school.

'It is now time for Safir class to receive their

badges. I am sure you all remember when you were young, taking your first steps in the Academy. To graduate from Safir class takes a lot of hard work – but as you know, once you've graduated, you can officially call yourself a genie. Please would Safir class make their way to the stage.'

Methuzular nodded to the orchestra and they struck up the tune again. The assembled genies applauded as, one by one, Jamie and his friends shook Methuzular's hand. The genie headmaster smiled and pointed at a place on their waistcoats. As he did so, a badge magically appeared on them. It was orange with a picture of a

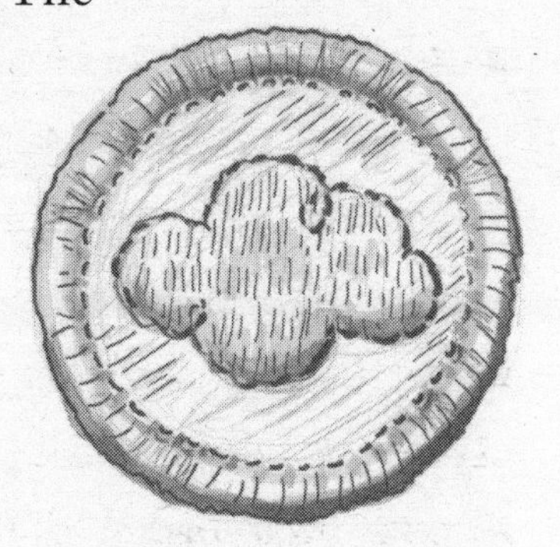

cloud in the middle stitched in gleaming gold thread. Jamie examined the badge proudly as he returned to his seat.

Methuzular cleared his throat and called for silence once again. 'We do have another small matter to deal with,' he said. 'Jamie Najar has become a genie, which means his wish has been granted. That means I can perform one more duty.'

Methuzular nodded to Balthazar who stood and took the stage. 'Balthazar Najar,' Methuzular said, smiling, 'you are now to re-join your clan and work with them to grant wishes. Live lightly and shine brightly, my friend.'

Methuzular took a deep breath and blew a wish to Balthazar. When Balthazar emerged from the cloud of sparkles his tatty green overalls had been replaced by a brilliant red Najar waistcoat. The genies clapped and cheered and out of the corner of his eye, Jamie saw Clampfinger

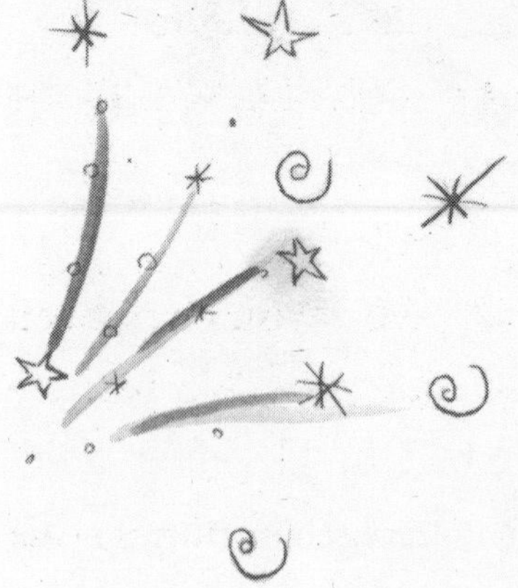

wiping a tear away. Balthazar grinned and waved happily to the crowd. As he made his way down from the stage, he tripped on his new pantaloons and tumbled towards the floor, but somehow Balthazar managed to turn the fall into an elegant tumble and landed on his feet bowing like a gymnast. Methuzular shook his head as Balthazar flashed the laughing genies a winning smile.

Before Methuzular dismissed the school, he made them all recite the Genie Code. For the first time Jamie joined in, knowing that, as a genie himself now, he had to live by the rules too.

Once the ceremony was over, Adeel and Jamie made their way back to the dorm.

'Well, see you next term, then,' said Adeel.

Jamie felt his heart sink. 'I don't know if I'll be coming back, Adeel,' he said.

'But you have to!' gasped Adeel.

Jamie shook his head. 'My wish has been granted, Balthazar is safe. I don't need to be here any more.'

Adeel looked at his friend with sad eyes. 'We shall all miss you,' he said quietly.

'I won't!' said Dabir. 'Good riddance, if you ask me. You've caused me nothing but trouble. My hands smell like dusters from all the lamps I've had to polish, and grooming the magic carpets takes so long that I've started to sleep in the hay.'

'You brought that on yourself, Dabir,' said Adeel angrily.

Dabir snorted. 'I shouldn't have been punished for trying to do everyone a favour. This lot may think you're a real genie, but you'll always be a human to me! You might have managed to scrape through the exam, but you'll never be as good as us.'

Jamie had finally had enough. There was one thing he wanted to do before he left the Academy and as a proper genie he was now allowed to do it. 'Dabir Ganim,' he said, 'I challenge you to a magic carpet race, genie to genie.'

Adeel gasped. No genie could back down from a challenge. It was rule number three of the Genie Code.

'If I win,' said Jamie, 'you have to accept that I am a proper genie and shake me by the hand.'

'And if you lose,' said Dabir, 'everyone will know that you're not as good as us. It will be fun to send you back home with your tail between your legs, human. In fact, if I win, I'll even give you one.'

Word of the challenge spread quickly through the Academy and as Dabir and Jamie waited at the racetrack, it seemed like every genie in the school had gathered to watch. They were to go once around the track – the winner was the first genie to cross the finish line.

Dabir clambered up on Viper and Jamie jumped aboard Threadbare. Jamie knew he was good at flying his carpet – he just hoped he had the skills to beat Dabir.

Adeel blew the starter whistle and the race began. Jamie and Threadbare hurtled towards the first bend. Dabir was shocked by the speed Jamie went on Threadbare and took a moment to catch up, but by the time they got to the first jump, Jamie was still in the lead. Dabir and Viper pulled up alongside him.

'I'm going to teach you your first proper lesson about magic carpet racing,' hissed Dabir. 'Never play fair.'

When they were out of sight of the crowd, Dabir reached over and yanked one of Threadbare's tassels. The carpet bucked in shock and Jamie was thrown off, landing on the ground in a tangle of limbs. Dabir cackled and zoomed

on. Jamie picked himself up and shook his head. He couldn't let Dabir get away with that. Threadbare doubled back and scooped him up.

'Come on, boy,' whispered Jamie. 'Let's show them what we've got.'

Threadbare whizzed eagerly after Dabir. When they came around the corner, Jamie saw Dabir in the distance. He had slowed down to mock Jamie, confident of victory. Jamie decided to try a new tactic he'd been working on. He carefully leant forward and lay down flat on the carpet. With his rider in this streamlined position, Threadbare began to pick up speed, faster and faster, until the world slipped past them in a blur. Dabir hadn't noticed anything going on behind him. Silently they began to gain on the nasty genie.

When the crowd saw what was going on they started cheering. Everyone knew how mean Dabir was and they were pleased if the new genie could teach him a lesson. Dabir looked behind him but all he could see was Threadbare – Jamie was too flat to be seen. Dabir smirked, thinking that Jamie was still in the bushes, and arrogantly presumed the crowd were cheering for him and began to wave back.

With Jamie's clever streamlining, he and Threadbare were zooming faster than ever and they whistled towards the finish line like a rocket. As he passed by, Jamie managed to give a shocked-looking Dabir a smile and a little wave. By the time Dabir realised what was happening, it was too late. Jamie sat up on his knees just in time to zip across the finish line and claim victory as his genie friends cheered and gathered all around him to celebrate.

CHAPTER 18

On the way back to school, all the genies were talking about the brilliant move Jamie had pulled, and how sulky Dabir had looked when he was forced to shake Jamie's hand at the end.

As they passed Methuzular's office, the headmaster beckoned Jamie inside. 'Back in your home your parents are waking. They'll notice that you have gone if you don't return soon.'

Jamie nodded. It was time for him to go.

Methuzular placed a hand on his shoulder. 'You'll always be welcome back, Jamie. We genies keep an eye on everything you humans get up to. Wish for it hard enough and one of us will see.'

Jamie nodded again. He felt sad leaving, but he missed his old life too much, and didn't want to worry his parents. Knowing that he could come back if he wanted to made him feel a little happier, though.

'There is one more thing,' said Methuzular. 'When you first arrived at the Academy I looked into your eyes and thought I saw a glimmer of someone I recognised staring back at me.'

Jamie was confused. 'I don't understand.'

Methuzular held up a finger – he wasn't finished. 'Now that you have passed your exam with double points, I am certain of it. You do have genie blood, Jamie Najar. One of your relatives was once a genie. They chose to leave this world behind forever and wished themselves human.'

'Can genies do that?' said Jamie.

'Oh yes,' Methuzular replied. 'It very rarely happens and of course there is no return, but this

genie fell in love with a human. They decided to sacrifice everything they knew as a genie and become human themselves so that they could live with that person for the rest of their life.'

Jamie's mind was racing once again. He thought of his mum and dad. He couldn't believe that either of them had ever been a genie!

'Who is it, Methuzular? Tell me!'

'I can't,' said Methuzular quietly. 'She will tell you herself when she is ready. Perhaps she already has.'

Jamie gasped. 'She?'

Methuzular shook his head. 'I have said too much. We must get you home.'

Methuzular had just closed his eyes and was beginning to draw breath when Jamie spotted Balthazar and Adeel running towards them.

'Wait!' shouted Balthazar.

Methuzular opened his eyes and let the wish pass.

'I thought I'd missed you,' said Balthazar, as he panted to a stop. 'We haven't said goodbye!'

Jamie gave his friends a hug. 'Thanks for everything,' he told them, and really meant it.

Balthazar laughed. '*I* should be thanking *you*!

You've set me free and now I can return to my clan!'

'Poor them,' said Methuzular, with a wink.

Jamie smiled as Balthazar shook him firmly by the hand. 'Live lightly and shine brightly, my friend.'

'I'll miss you too!' said Adeel, hugging Jamie. 'But I won't miss your snoring!'

'It really is time to go, Jamie,' said Methuzular gently, already drawing breath again.

And as Jamie was shrouded in sparkles, he saw his friends slowly fade and felt the familiar dizziness sweep over him.

When he opened his eyes, he was back in his bedroom wearing his ordinary clothes. Paulie's poster was still stuck to the wall and the teapot lay on the floor where he had left it. Jamie peered under the bed. The Formula One trophy he had won was still there and so too was a bowl of never-ending ice cream. Jamie smiled.

At that moment, his alarm clock sounded.

He couldn't believe he had to get ready for another day at

school already. When he opened his wardrobe he gasped in surprise. Hanging there was his genie outfit! Jamie stroked the silk waistcoat. Maybe he'd wear it again one day.

Downstairs in the kitchen, his mum, dad and Baby Paulie were having breakfast. Baby Paulie was dribbling mashed up banana down his chin and his dad was struggling with the crossword. Jamie watched them for a moment. The Academy and the genies had been incredible, but he'd really missed his family too. Jamie surprised them all with fierce hugs before snatching a slice of toast – he was running late.

As he was going out, his gran came down the stairs. 'Off to school?' she asked.

Jamie nodded and noticed for the first time that her ears were ever so slightly pointy.

'Well, have a good day,' she said, her voice following him out of the door. 'And remember, whatever happens, live lightly and shine brightly.'

Jamie's eyes went wide. He decided that when he got back, he and his gran were going to have a very long talk.

Coming soon . . .

There's big trouble in the genie town of Lampville-upon-Cloud, and Balthazar needs his human friend Jamie to come back and help!

The bad genies have taken over, thrown the old headmaster of the Genie Academy in jail and are planning to take over the human world. But what can Jamie do about it? And with mean wishes being granted all over the place, how will they avoid being turned into figburgers – or worse?! It's going to take more than magic to put things right . . .

Another hilarious story by CBBC's Ciaran Murtagh.

WISHING FOR MORE?

Come and explore
the Genie Academy website
for fun and games,
book news and much, much more!

GENIEACADEMY.CO.UK

Also by Ciaran Murtagh:

DINOPANTS

Caveboy Charlie Flint is fed up with dinosaurs leaving poo all over his home town of Sabreton – so Charlie invents dinopants!

But how will he convince the dinosaurs to put on his dinopants? And what about the terrifying T-Rex who is determined to make both the pants and Charlie extinct?

DINOPOO

Charlie's new invention – a loo for dinosaurs – is angering the giant millipedes who live underground, and whose home is filling up with dinopoo. Charlie soon finds himself pitted against the fearsome king of the millipedes and in a very sticky situation!

DINOBURPS

Charlie's tasty fizzy drink for dinosaurs has an unexpected side-effect: smelly dinoburps!

When the town is swamped in their smelly gas, Charlie has to make a dangerous journey through the jungle, across the sea and to a volcano to get the remedy. And even worse – with a girl.

DINOBALL

When his pet dinosaur joins in a game of football, Charlie has an idea for a whole new sport: dinoball!

A dinoball cup is set up with local villages, but when the games begin, some of the teams are getting a little bit too competitive . . .